DREX

HEIDI HARRIS

Heidi Harris

First Publication 2016

Cover design by Delilah Gose

To A-M,

I'm glad you have been a part of my life.

I love you cuz!

Thank you God, for helping me

finish this book and sending people along the way to encourage

me to finish.

"A good name is to be chosen rather than great riches,
Loving favor rather than silver and gold.

The rich and the poor have this in common,
The LORD is the maker of them all.

A prudent man foresees evil and hides himself,
But the simple pass on and are punished.

By humility and the fear of the LORD
Are riches and honor and life.

Thorns and snares are in the way of the perverse;
He who guards his soul will be far from them.

Train up a child in the way he should go,
And when he is old he will not depart from it.

The rich rules over the poor,
And the borrower is servant to the lender.

He who sows iniquity will reap sorrow,
And the rod of his anger will fail.

He who has a generous eye will be blessed,
For he gives of his bread to the poor.

Cast out the scoffer, and contention will leave;
Yes, strife and reproach will cease.

He who loves purity of heart
And has grace on his lips,
The king will be his friend."

Proverbs 22:1-11 (NKJV)

Proverbs has a lot of wisdom. I want to have a good name. I want to stand for something. I want who I am to mean something to those around me.

A lot of people in your life are going to try to mold you into something. It may be negative or positive. I hope you choose to be someone of integrity, like this scripture says.

Time Difference Reference

Time Difference Reference

Zelle	=	Jareneiks (Deltik)
1 month	=	1 year
15 days	=	6 months
5 days	=	2 months
1 day	=	12 days
2 hours	=	1 day
1 hour	=	12 hours
5 min	=	1 hour
1 min	=	12 min.

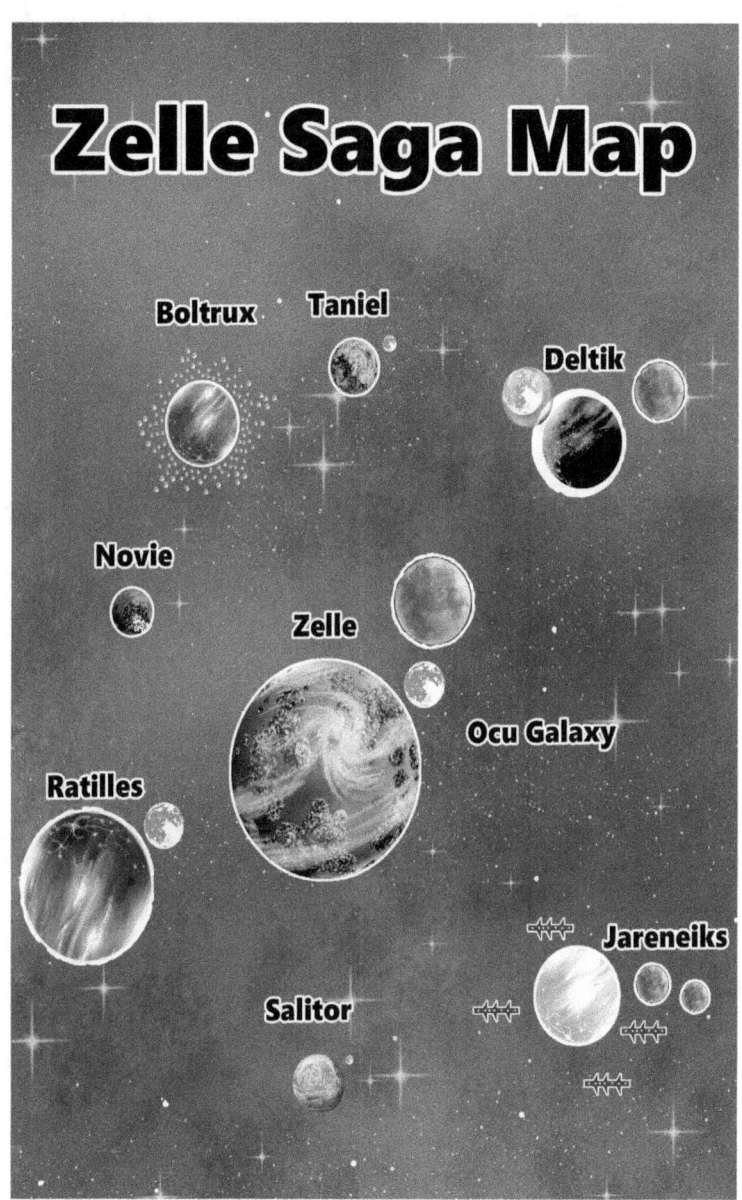

9

PROLOGUE

"I wish Mom were here." I sulked in the bulky red chair.

"I know, bud." Dad froze in place for a second. "Me too."

"I know we have to wait, but..." I sighed.

"We'll find your mom as soon as we can, Jon." Dad's voice was melancholy.

Dad was always willing to talk about Mom. When he did, an overwhelming wave of Triz always hit. Some of his thoughts and emotions he kept from us, but the sadness was impossible to hide. Usually his Triz were happy, sadness, frustration, and a lot of guilt.

"Dad, don't take this the wrong way, but..." I paused.

He turned and gave me his full attention. "But what?"

"Why Mom?" I asked.

"Why what?" Dad's eyebrow rose.

"I guess what I meant is, why did you marry Mom?"

Dad grinned. "You don't want to hear that boring stuff."

He hit me on top of the head with his papers and left the room.

That was his way of saying you can continue the conversation if you want to come with me. Dad was always doing that. He always had somewhere to go or something to do. I got up and matched his steps. He went to his study and started filing the papers in his hand.

I leaned against the door frame. "Dad…" I drew out his name.

He closed the drawer. "So you were serious." He grinned teasingly.

I rolled my eyes. He sat on the desk. I plopped into the chair and spun around. I had the coolest Dad. He was happy to have me or my sisters' tag along with him.

"I met Miranda about twelve years ago." He laughed, and I did too. "It was kind of embarrassing." He warned.

"Sweet, those are the best kind." I grinned.

"Jon." He accused.

"Sorry Dad." I bit back my smile.

"It was the first time I had seen Miranda. I was visiting a friend, and he invited me to come with him to her birthday party. The yard was lit up. It was just getting dark out. I kept my eyes on Miranda most of the night when finally he dared me to ask her to take a walk." Dad smiled.

"You talked to Mom on a dare?" I asked.

"Yeah, but that isn't the embarrassing part." He chuckled.

"What happened?" I asked.

"She said yes. We went for a walkout by the creek. It had rained a few days before and it was a little muddy. I slipped and fell knee deep in the water." Dad's face was full of mock horror.

"No!" I laughed.

"Yes." He laughed too. "She had pity on me and we went on a date the next night. We got married, and you three came."

1

Joe wrapped his arms around my sister's waist and set his chin on her shoulder. Being around them gave me the same feeling as chugging syrup. I liked Joe. He was good for Jahni, almost as good as she was for him. A little over three years ago, they came barging into my world and rearranged it.

Morie and Popsie were good to me, and my twin sister Rose, but I loved Jahni and Joe too. Living with the Ratillians hadn't been that bad. They wouldn't let us go anywhere, so it was a lot like being kept in a large cage.

Although I pretended to act disgusted every time they acted like this, I wanted it too. The happy family and beautiful wife on my side sounded like a life I could live with. Joe really was a lucky guy.

"Why don't you two get a room?" I complained.

"We have one." Joe grinned.

No one could mistake the unshakable love in my sister's eyes as she gazed back into his. I groaned. I couldn't stand it anymore, so I headed outside. A walk would be good for me. My long legs reluctantly stumbled down each step. I watched the stones move past in a blur. I wandered down toward the entrance.

"Hi Rose." I mumbled.

She giggled. I glanced at her. Her smile was as sparkling as always. She was contagious. My lips went up in a half grin.

"And I thought I had been quiet." She smiled an almost pout.

I shook my head and grinned bigger. A few guards saluted us before they opened the gate. Rose saluted them back.

[I should have gone out the back way.] I complained to Rose.

[No. This is fun.] Rose grinned at the guards.

One of the younger guards let a brief smile escape. He was only a year older than we were. I walked faster so she would have to catch up.

[You're going to give him ideas if you keep it up.] I warned her with my thoughts.

She beamed. [That might be the idea.]

Oh great, first Jahni now Rose! Sisters! I grunted. She laughed and started humming. I liked to hear her hum. We didn't say anything for quite a while. We never needed to. Rose knew me better than anyone did. She probably knew I was heading for this walk before I did.

16

Rose started climbing a tree beside the path, so I did too. She lay back on a limb and looked at the sky. There wasn't a cloud in the sky.

"It's beautiful." She sighed in satisfaction.

I tried to see it through her eyes. It was nice, but my mind wasn't on Zelle. I was starting to feel stressed.

"What is it?" Rose's head twirled in my direction.

"Mom." I let the word fall from my lips.

[Oh!] She knew immediately.

We needed to leave for MaCownia soon. It has been three years since the last meteor storm. Finally, we could make it through to Drex. I don't want to go. I like being here with Rose, Dad, Jahni, and Joe. Leaving might change things. Last time I was gone with Rose and I almost didn't make it back. Before that, the land died. What if we died? It was possible; the MaCownians were ruthless. Well, most of them were. I grinned as Hálie's blue eyes and blonde hair crossed my mind. She sure was cute. Hálie had shared a cell with Jahni for a few hours. Maybe returning to MaCownia wouldn't be so bad.

Jahni asked Dad once, how the land had changed so fast? She came here once when everything was dead, and the next week when we all returned, it looked like it does now. Dad told her it was part of the magic in the land. As long as the youngest royal is on Zelle, it stays beautiful and flourishes, but if the child leaves, the planet starts dying after four days.

I'm not sure whether Rose is older or I am. It doesn't matter to me. Although, I'm sure she'd like to be older. Two weeks after we came back, Rose asked Dad the question. She wanted to know which one of us happened to be older. Dad said he wasn't sure.

"I was just happy you both were here and safe. But your mother knows." He had added.

He used knows in the present tense. We all chose to believe Mom is out there on Drex. She had to be one of their 'art pieces' on display. They collected people from various planets and put them in museums.

I pulled a leaf off the tree and proceeded to rip it to shreds. I felt the time passing. Rose curled down the tree. I threw down the stem of the leaf and climbed down too.

"You know it'll be okay, right?" Rose asked.

I nodded my head slowly. She smiled and began humming as we headed back. The sky was growing dark when we reached the front door.

[Finally, they're here!] Dad exclaimed.

I wasn't ready for this. It was time to come up with the

strategy. I barely budged.

[It's not what you think.] Rose grabbed my hand and pulled me into our most used sitting room.

Jahni was sitting on a couch while Joe's arm draped around her shoulder. Dad sat across from them in a large chair. I crashed on the couch next to Joe, and Rose curled in a chair near Dad.

"We have some good news and bad news." Jahni twisted her hands together.

"Okay?" I asked, and Rose leaned in.

"I'll take the bad news first." Dad said dryly.

"Jahni can't go to MaCownia or…" Joe spoke. Jahni thought something to him and smiled.

"Why not?" I wanted to know.

It was bad enough leaving home, but to do it without my oldest sister? No way! It wasn't like Jahni to bail out on her responsibilities.

She smiled at me. This was very unlike her. I didn't understand why she was so happy and calm. She loved adventure. To stay home when she could be racing off to fight off the Drecians was so not Jahni. And if Jahni didn't go, neither would Joe. My stomach tightened.

"I have to stay." Jahni said.

"Now for the good news!" Joe was ecstatic.

"Sloane!" She jabbed him in the ribs gently.

Dad was solemn. I did sense his mental wall go up in a flash. He didn't say a word.

"Well…" Rose said in excitement.

My head turned sharply to Rose. Why was she getting excited? Rose ignored me, focusing her eyes on Jahni. Reluctantly, I did the same.

"The youngest member of the bloodline has to stay on Zelle." Her words rushed out and tumbled over each other.

But Rose and I are…It dawned on me as Rose's thoughts exploded. Each one was about a baby. Jahni was pregnant and Rose was hugging her. I was going to be an uncle. Dad was going to be a Grandpa. And we were going to have to do this very important mission alone. Great! One worry down, Zelle would be safe. A million and two surfaced. I closed my eyes to take them in.

Rose's giggles danced in the air. I stood up and walked out. I felt their stares as I left. I didn't want to pretend with Mom's fate on my 17-year-old shoulders.

[Congrats Jahni. You'll be a good Mom.] I thought to my sister.

"Thanks." She startled me.

My steps came to a halt. Jahni caught me off guard like no one else. It was hard to see her coming. I knew where Rose was almost always. If she was sad in her room, I knew. That didn't happen often, but on occasion, it did.

Dad's Triz are different. A Triz is a thought or feeling people from Zelle can sense. This includes their descendants that are born on other planets. He isn't as easy to read as Rose is, but within thirty yards, readable. Joe, well Sloane, if you're talking to Jahni, is harder. Maybe it is because he's not blood, or maybe because he is married to Jahni.

"You're welcome." I mumbled.

"You okay?" Her voice was gentle.

Crap! She is getting as good at reading me as Rose. Jahni has kind of taken on the mother role since we have been back. Not the clean your room now! But the small questions that make you think and consider why. Most of the time, it involves guilt. This was one of those times. You okay, means that I should have stayed, held out my hand to Joe, teased Dad about being a Grandpa, and hugged Jahni. I leaned back against the wall.

"Just thinkin' 'bout Mom." I grumbled.

She nodded graciously. I feigned a smile. She saw through it.

[You'll make a good uncle, you know.] She stated.

[I guess.] I gave her a weak hug. [Love you Jahni.]

[Love you, Jon.] She hugged me tighter. When she let go, her smile was bright as she returned to the rest of the family.

"What was that all about?" Dad asked her when she returned.

I closed my eyes and told myself to breathe. I didn't want to do this without her. The last time we went to MaCownia, Jahni ended up on the auction block. Truthfully, I respected her for it. She was the reason it wasn't Rose…or me. Without her? I just don't know.

We have to go through MaCownia to fuel up. There is no getting around that. I groaned and headed upstairs.

Later that night, I was in my room. I heard a knock. I rolled over to face the door.

"Come in." I said.

Joe surprised me by walking in. I gave him a dirty look. "What do you want?" He was unphased. At least he couldn't read me. That was something. He didn't say anything while he stood looking at me mercilessly.

"Well." I drew out the word. This silence was unnerving in a way that made me curious.

He smiled.

"Fine. Sit down." I growled.

I looked off to my right. The wall was full of posters of Shuttle Cars, including a picture of all of us with the old Vaktow. I kept him in my vision. He sat down across from me. What in the world brought this on?

Finally, he broke the silence. [Jahni's been thinking about you a lot.]

I turned and gave him a sharp look to hide my guilt. I hated Jahni worrying about me. He ignored my look again. Was this man made of steel! Jeesh!

[I thought you'd be psyched to drive one of the newer ships.] He grinned and gave a brief look at the posters. I leaned back with my hands behind me to prop my body up.

"It's not that." I responded.

"Then what?" He spoke aloud too.

I didn't like where this was going. Too serious. It was one thing to whine to Rose, which I did too much, or even Jahni, but Joe. Not feeling it. Nothing. After two minutes, the silence was killing me. This guy's patience level was ridiculous; it would make me feel better if he yelled at me. But no, he was Mr. Quiet ugg. I rolled my eyes.

"Are you ready to leave yet?" I sat up.

"Not by a long shot." He growled.

My eyes shot to his eyes in utter shock. He was leaning toward me with too intense eyes. Maybe he had less patience than I thought.

"Fine! It's your life, spend it however you want." I crashed on my bed and closed my eyes. I felt his eyes seething into my skin.

23

I peeked at him out of the corner of my eye. He hadn't moved. I fought back the groan in my throat.

[Dude! Leave!] That was plain.

He could get the point. I was kind of surprised one of my sisters hadn't butted in yet. They had to feel my involuntary Triz.

[Did she send you?] I forced anger into each word, referring to Jahni.

[No.] He clipped.

[So why bother?] I asked. Despite myself, I was slightly curious why he was putting up with me.

[You've been...] He paused. [No one needs the world on their shoulders. Zelle's going to be fine. Siah will see to that.]

I sat up. "What? Who is Siah?"

He looked sheepish. "I think it's a boy."

"Does Jahni know you already named the kid Josiah?" If not, he was going to get it. I laughed.

"Kind of." Joe replied.

That's a no. "I hope I'm there when you face the Queen's wrath, believe me it's not pretty." I spouted.

He laughed too. "Don't I know it."

Maybe he's not perfect after all. He looked at me expectantly. I'm running out of excuses. I could jet out of here, but it is my room and he could catch me easily on the way out. So it's silence or give. Obviously, I can't handle the silence. I guess that's why I like to hear Rose hum mindlessly. It fills the silence.

[Do you ever give up?] I asked.

[Nope.] He answered.

I glared. I must be worse at this than I thought. Or maybe they're becoming immune. That would be my luck. I have to think up some new tactics. Sleeping, that could be a tactic! I stripped off my shirt, threw at Joe, and rolled over to hug my pillow. A second later, he threw it back at me, hard.

Three minutes later, I couldn't take it anymore! I wish Rose were asleep; sometimes she hums in her dreams. If I had that to concentrate on, I could outlast him, but it's way too quiet. I thought about asking her to hum, but that'd be lame, really lame.

[You coming to MaCownia with us?] I caved.

[I don't know. Why?] Joe asked.

I debated. I had better get it over with. [Just wonderin', I just thought since Jahni you know.]

"You were worried I wouldn't go with you?" Joe asked incredulously. "That's what all this is about?"

I turned over to see him. "Well yeah, you got skill. I always thought Jahni would come too, you know?"

He nodded. The stunned reaction had left his face, but it hadn't left his eyes. "I'm not sure what I'll want to do about Jahni." He said carefully. "We were younger than you are now, when we did what we did."

I nodded a yes, not meaning it.

"Jahni didn't know what was going on until it was over. I had an outline from Uncle Adeam." He smiled. "But I was winging it too. The trick is being flexible and not getting caught."

"That simple." I spit out.

"Jon, you know everything about engines." Joe told me earnestly.

"I guess." I stared at the floor and let them drift around.

"I'm trying to give you a compliment." Joe's voice deepened.

I took my eyes from my lap.

"And man, you're fast." Joe continued.

I grinned. Since I hit my growth spurt, no one can outrun me. That was a big plus.

"And Rose is on your side. She can charm her way out of the most difficult situations." Joe added.

"Yeah, she sure has a knack for that." I thought of all the times she gave a sweet smile and got whatever she asked for.

"If." He stressed. "I stay, you can handle it, especially with Rose with you."

I nodded, but this time I took his words more seriously. He got up to leave. That hadn't been as bad as I expected.

"Thanks… Sloane." I teased.

He grinned. "Later Robbie."

I threw an extra pillow at him. The door closed too fast, and it landed on the floor. He knew I didn't like being called by my middle name. Even worse, he called me Robbie as if I was a little kid. Jerk! I slammed back into bed. Pain! My head ached from the impact of the headboard. I grabbed the back of my head to check for blood. I found none.

"Ow. That hurts. Really hurts." I punched the bed with my right hand. "Crap." Slowly, I placed my head on the pillow. Pain sucks.

2

The sun hadn't been up long. I couldn't help my yawn as I stretched. My head hurt a little on the pillow, but I'd live. I glanced around the room and groaned. It was about time to start waking Rose. I had to coax her awake every morning for as long as I can remember.

[Rose.] She was out. It always took her forever to wake up.

[Breakfast is started.] Jahni told me.

[Thanks.] I stayed where I was, too comfortable to move far.

Jahni has the same problem I do. When the bright light comes on, we both wake up. I need darker curtains. Five minutes later, I threw on a shirt from the floor and headed downstairs.

"Nice look." Jahni's voice hinted at a hidden laugh.

"Yeah." Just because my shirt is wrinkled, I have sleep in my eyes, and I probably need a shave doesn't mean a thing.

[Hey Rose, you might want to get up, food's about ready.]

She started dreaming. That's a good sign.

"Rose coming?" Joe grinned. I mean Sloane-hmm, let's see if that bothers him.

"Twelve minutes… Sloane." I taunted.

His eyes snapped to mine with a half glare. Hmm, he doesn't like that. I was happy. Jahni caught the tension in the air. It was just enough to notice something was up.

"Okay?" Jahni asked. I shrugged my shoulders.

[Rose!] I thought louder.

[I'm up!] Rose countered.

[Sure you are.] I stressed each word.

[I am!] Rose yelled.

Twelve minutes later, Rose sat down, hair brushed with fresh clothes.

"Looking good!" Rose looked at me and commented.

"So I'm told." I grumbled, but wasn't mad. I knew I was trashed, but this is breakfast, so who really cares?

"Right on time…Robert." Joe...Sloane used my middle name in revenge.

[What's going on Jon?] Rose was concerned.

[Ugg. Don't worry 'bout it. I have been calling him Sloane.] I grinned.

[You didn't?] Rose was stunned.

[Rose, you know me.] I thought casually.

[So you did.] Rose thought placidly. [I'm surprised you're alive.]

[We'll see.] I was nonchalant.

"What can I say, Sloane." The tone in my voice was mocking him. "I know Rose."

"What's going on?" Dad took his place at the table and the food came.

"Nothing." I muttered.

"I was just challenging Robbie to a Zanxtear Race." He didn't bother veiling his threat.

"That's not fair!" I blurted out.

I gritted my teeth. I hated being called Robbie, and Joe knew it. Joe held the record for the best Zanxtear race in all of Zelle. He has been the reigning champion for the past three years.

A Zanxtear Race is the ultimate race. Not only does it require speed, but intelligence. A normal Zanxtear Race is based on speed (usually a two-mile run or more), agility (the run is through a forest. It's marked, but no path.) Knowledge (each contestant has their own Vaktow to work on with the same mechanical issue. It can be as simple as a wire being disconnected in the control panel or as complex as a turbine.

Once you're done with that, you swim a half a mile or more across a pool, pond, or down a river, where you will be given a test. It contains ten questions. The questions are designed to work your brain strategically. You will respond to the question with the best solution for every situation listed.

In order to pass the test, you must get a seven. If you get less than seven, you get a second chance. When you retake it, they tell you one question that was right and one that was wrong. Normally, you have one shot at the test, because the others finish before you get a chance to complete your redo.

It generally takes one to seven hours to finish the race. It depends on what is wrong with the Vaktow and the test questions. A few decades ago, the Zanxtear Race of all Zanxtear Races happened. It took 7 days.

James K. Williams, Aaron L. Peterson, Michael L. Alan, and Joshua J. Jones spent four months training for it. In the end, it came down to the test. Jones finished the test first and failed. He also failed the second test. About that time, Williams failed his first test too. Then Peterson and Alan showed up within a minute of each other.

Peterson passed the test the first time with a nine out of ten. Alan finished two minutes later with an eight. Jones passed with an eight the third time around and Williams came in last with a seven.

The whole stupid race came down to the strategy portion of the test. I closed my eyes. It would be a piece of cake to win the run. I could probably beat most when it came to the Vaktow portion of the race too. I was an average swimmer, but it wouldn't be more than a mile.

Joe was an excellent swimmer and an expert at finding the best strategies to solve any situation. More than that, he could put it into practice. He was an okay mechanic. Maybe okay wasn't enough credit, but I needed all the ego boost I can make up, if I had a chance to beat him or even come in a close second.

"What do you mean?" He attempted innocence. He lifted a forkful into his mouth and looked at me, so I could see his eyes dancing.

I participated in my first Zanxtear Race two years ago, but I came in fifteenth out of seventeen. It was the junior version. Last year went better. I came in fifth out of twenty-one. I haven't participated in the senior division once, and Joe has won it three times!

"What, you're not afraid of a little competition, are you?" Joe met my eyes with his dare.

Jahni looked at her husband and me suspiciously. She thought something to him. Rose's Triz were on edge. Everyone in Zalnorel knew about Joe's ability. Mine were posted as the upcoming Prince in the tabloids. Upcoming as in a few years, I might be a challenger. As in now, today, I had no hope.

"Of course I'm not afraid!" Crap! What am I going to do? Someone needs to bail me out of this!

"Good." His eyes were triumphant. "When would be good for you?"

Next year! "Whenever is cool." I seethed.

"Sure it is." He grinned wickedly.

He had me. There was no possible way I could win. What am I going to do when I lose? Suck it up, I guess. Rose gave me a wary look. She knew my chances and feelings about how it would go down. Maybe we could make it an open race. That way, I can at least beat someone and not seem so lame. I am getting better. I just haven't reached the best, yet.

"It has been a while since we have held a Zanxtear Race here, usually Landryn holds one." Dad said thoughtfully.

"I think we should let the other contestants know immediately." I slipped in.

Joe gave me a nod of approval. "Shooting for second?" He asked.

I ignored him. "What day?"

"I think three weeks from now will give them and us sufficient time to prepare." Dad answered. "I will take care of it after breakfast."

"Sounds good. Do you think Jasmine and Paul will make it?" Joe's eyes twinkled.

My cousin Jasmine came in second last year. Uncle Adeamkenrick is King of Landryn. She is one of the best

33

mechanics I have ever seen in action.

Paul isn't a cousin, but he shows up at the same functions. He is a couple of years older than Joe. He is cool. He came in third last year. Joe *would* invite them. The competition would be difficult enough without Jasmine and Paul. I would be lucky to come in fourth. Great!

"I don't see why not." Dad smiled. He had caught on to us by then.

[He is getting you good.] Rose commented. [This is worse than death.]

[I know.] I moaned. Her laughter swam through the room. Everyone looked at her.

"What?" Rose asked.

One thing I loved about Rose is her subtlety. She wouldn't betray me. Since I can't keep anything from her, ever, that is one of her best qualities.

"This will be your first senior Zanxtear Race." Jahni was thoughtful. "I'm sure you will do okay." She placed a kiss on the top of my head and sat in her chair.

"What about me!" Joe complained.

Jahni rolled her eyes. "You don't need luck."

I have three weeks to get ready for it. My worries about MaCownia shifted to the back of my thoughts. The next three weeks would zoom by. The question would be whether or not I would make a fool of myself? I don't know. I would like to beat Joe, but that was just too much to hope for. Maybe I could take 2nd or 3rd if I work at it.

"This came for you today. Jahni got it by mistake."

I grabbed the envelope from Rose's grasp. It had two words on the return address: Jasmine and underneath it was written Landryn in neat loops. I opened it quickly. Jasmine has never sent me anything in the mail before.

Jon,

I hear you're moving up to the Senior Division. I just wanted to wish you good luck. I'm sure you will do okay. This time I won't be able to cheer you on since I will be busy trying to win.

If you need any pointers, I'm your girl. See you in two weeks!

Jasmine

She's right. I will do okay, which is generally good when you're moving up a division. I didn't want to be just okay with Joe's challenge up in the air. I spent the past week using the

35

Magnesystem on my Com. It is a quick way to get information. It has a record of all the questions of past Zanxtear Races and diagrams of different Shuttle Cars, including the average Vaktows in most of the races. I compared present and past years until I could tell the differences easily. The Magnesystem is interactive, 3D, and efficient.

I ran into my office downstairs. I jotted down a quick note, stuffed it in an envelope, and sent it off.

Thanks Jaz,

See you in 10 days. Pray!

Jon

3

Knock. Knock. I looked at the window. It was still dark.

"Yeah." I grumbled. [Who is it?]

[Jahni.] My sister thought back.

"Coming." I walked over to the door, unlocked it, and let her in.

"Morning." Jahni waited.

"Yeah." I looked down where my Wrist Com normally is. Seeing my empty wrist, I realized it was still charging. Dumb technology. [Why couldn't the battery last for a month?]

"Great question. I will tell Sloane to get on that." Jahni grinned.

[He would be the one to do it.] I thought sarcastically.

Jahni's right eyebrow went up. "Are you okay?"

I yawned. "What time is it?" I avoided her question. I should be getting pumped for today's big race, instead I was reminded how well Joe does on everything. He was a problem solver. I remembered our conversation from last month. Okay, he was making it up, but he did it better than anyone else I knew with the exception of my sister Jahni.

"Twenty minutes before sunrise." Jahni told me.

I stretched and yawned and walked over to my bed and sat down. "Well, find a seat."

Jahni came over and sat on the couch by my bed. "Sloane really likes the name Siah. What do you think?"

"Seriously Jahni? That's what you want to talk about on one of the biggest days of my life?" I gaped at her, not sure if I was awake.

"No, but I got a legit sentence out of you." Jahni stretched out on the couch.

I bit my lip and tilted it to the left side of my face to refrain from exploding.

"Jon, chill." Jahni's eyes darted at me.

"Whatever." I shook my head slightly.

[I'm not in denial. I know Sloane challenged you.]

"Yeah, he did." I responded quickly.

"And you egged him on." Jahni looked at me knowingly.

"What?" I asked. "No, not me. Does that even sound like me?"

"Yep." Jahni laughed.

I shrugged.

"Regardless..." Jahni paused.

"Yeah?" I asked.

"You will always be my brother. I love you." Jahni stood up.

"You too." I frowned.

"Cheer up. Go out there and give Sloane a run for his money." Jahni laughed.

I laughed. "Really?"

"Yeah, I'm rooting for both of you." Jahni gave me a hug.

"Thanks sis." I smiled, even though I didn't want to. Jahni walked to the door. "Jahni?"

"Yes?" She paused.

"Siah is okay." I nodded.

"I think I like it too. Don't tell Sloane yet. I want to make him work for it." Jahni winked.

I laughed.

4

If Jasmine weren't my cousin, I'd be in line with the other five guys hanging on her every word. She is beautiful, has curves, loves machines, God, and competitions. On top of all that, she was intelligent.

She had a pair of jeans on, the tip of a clean grease rag hung out of her back pocket. A black belt hugged her hips with a star belt buckle. It was the crest of Landryn. She had on a black t-shirt with silver lettering that said 'I know I'm the princess.' I chuckled. That was so Jaz. She had an attitude. Her dark hair went halfway down her back. For the most part, it was straight. The ends always seemed to curl. Once we got started, she'd pull it back and get down to business.

Jasmine heard me laugh and turned in my direction. Her smile was huge and genuine. Her entourage turned to see what she was looking at.

"Jon!" Jasmine exclaimed, and left the five guys gawking at her as she walked to me.

They were wondering what the kid had that they didn't. I smiled back. They didn't know the 'kid' was her cousin. Apparently, they don't keep up with the tabloids. They thought I was competition. I liked that.

"Hey Jaz." I gave her a hug.

"You nervous?" Jaz asked.

[Yeah.] I answered her.

I looked at the crowd. They moved through the streets like a river. Jasmine put a hand on my shoulder. My eyes shot back to her face.

[Hey, I was too my first time. No worries.] Jaz grinned.

"Yeah right." I rolled my eyes. "No big deal."

She flashed a grin. [Tell you what, you can come in second and I'll come in first. Joseph can take third. Sound good?]

I couldn't help but grin back. She sure was an optimist, and it was catching. "Sounds perfect."

The competitors had their own posse. Two tough guys traveled together not 20 yards away. They wore dark matching jackets meant to make them look intimidating. They were scoping out the competition, others like Jasmine, had fan clubs. Some hung out with their siblings, working through the crowds together.

A brother and younger sister sat on some steps looking

down at Jasmine and me. The boy was older. He was giving her some advice. A few were loners, no fan club, or friends watching their backs. I searched the crowd for Paul. It had been hours and I still couldn't find him.

I tried to remember who came in fourth last year. My mind was blank. We had been so hyped up Joe won and Jaz hit second I forgot the rest.

Jasmine's groupies were getting irritated. They were about to make their way over. I couldn't help smiling at their irritation.

[Look at that loser!] The guy with the black t-shirt thought to the other guys. He didn't realize I could hear every thought.

[Jerk!] The one with the blue shirt bellowed.

[I think we can take him out.] The third said.

He was more muscular than the rest, and had the beginnings of a serious beard coming in. His dark hair hovered past his eyebrows. His brown eyes looked dangerous. The other two didn't say anything, but their glares come in loud and clear.

"Um!" I searched my brain for a decent excuse. There was no way I could take on five lovesick *men* defending *their territory*. "I need to find Sloane."

Jasmine grinned wickedly. "Sloane, huh? I tried that *once*. I can't believe Joseph actually lets you get away with that."

42

My lips twitched upward. "Yeah. He hates it."

"You've got a death wish." She shook her head, but the pride held in her eyes. I slipped a few feet away.

"Well, we are holding the first Zanxtear Race in years for a reason." I grinned.

Her grin slipped in to shock. "You're kidding!"

"Nope." I gestured with my hands. "All me."

[He challenged you to a Zanxtear Race.] She thought incredulously.

"Afraid so." I forced a light tone into my voice. I trailed a few steps away. [I'd say good luck, but…]

[Yeah. I know.] Jasmine thought back.

"Later Jaz!" I raised my voice.

"See you when you finish." Jasmine grinned.

I knew what Jaz meant. She was planning on finishing before me in the race and she had the experience. The truth is, she probably will beat me to the finish line. I forced adrenaline through my system. I could do this! Maybe. I turned away in search of Joe. He'd know where Paul was, if he came. Who am I kidding? He had to be here somewhere.

[Not if I see you first Jaz.] I thought back.

I heard a faint laugh in the background as I pushed my way through the crowd. I thought about asking Jahni where Joe was, but threw it away immediately. Rose was hanging out with a

43

few of her friends at the house for a few hours, so she wouldn't know where to find Joe or Paul.

Joe looked up. He saw me and smiled. [Hi Jon.]

"Hi." [Sloane.] I said, as I got closer.

[Oh really.] Joe wasn't mad, but intense. I don't think I have the kind of commitment it takes to be that intense about anything.

[Don't be so cynical, you do just fine.] Rose encouraged.

She must have just arrived. I could almost feel her eyes roll. She always says I'm too hard on myself.

[Rose doing okay?] Joe asked.

"Yeah." I responded. He knew I had been talking to her, but not the topic. That is one good thing about being born a royal in Zalnorel.

"Paul finally showed up." Joe fiddled with some parts.

"He did." My voice sounded glum to my own ears. There goes third.

"Looks like God had mercy on you." Joe told me.

"What are you talking about?" He had lost me.

At that moment, Paul came around the corner juggling two drinks. His left arm was in a cast. My eyes widened. There's

44

hope! He handed a cup to Joe, who thanked him.

"Man, what happened to your arm?" I asked.

Paul grinned. "There's this girl, Bessica. She is so hott! Well, I climbed up on this shed to jump into this pool. Cause we were swimming." He winked at me.

I shook my head, but couldn't help my smile. The guy had guts, or stupidity. I wasn't sure which.

"And jumped in. Well, most of me did." Paul held up his arm. "It landed on the side of the pool. Concrete."

"Ouch." I winced. "That had to hurt."

"Yeah!" He walked over. "But check it." He held out his injured arm.

There were about fifty signatures, but in the middle, in big bold letters was written: *Come over any time* ☺ ♥ *Bessica*

I patted him on the back. "Good for you!" Good for me! Thank you Bessica!

"Shame about the race." Joe eyed me.

"Yeah." A note of sadness was in Paul's voice that spoke volumes. "Maybe next year I guess." He mumbled. "But I hope you two place." He grinned at Joe, then turned his head my way. "You might have a chance now." He teased me.

"Gee thanks." I muttered. Yes! I shouldn't be this excited about Paul's broken arm. I shoved the minimal guilt away easily. Yes! Yes! Yes!

45

[What's up?] Rose's thought was curious. She noticed my mood change immediately.

[Um, Paul broke his arm.] I confessed.

[Jon!] Rose chided.

[Yeah. I know, but I can't help it. I might actually place!] Excitement rolled through me.

[Is he okay?] Rose asked.

[Yeah, yeah, he just can't join the race.] I assured her.

[Okay.] Rose thought back.

Rose wasn't mad. So I let myself be happy again. There is a chance!

5

I had signed in, changed my clothes, and my tools were by the broken Vaktow. Jasmine had one main rule win it. Come to the race, get it right the first time, especially if it takes a minute more. The minute more is why she placed second last year instead of fifth or worse. A few screws were loose; it would have backfired when she went to start the engine that is if she hadn't checked it.

Joe's advice had been simple; Go faster than everyone else and do it right. Paul even pitched in. Find Joe and beat him. He had laughed afterwards.

I took a deep breath. I was as ready as I would be this year. I walked toward the starting line. This year's race had nineteen entries. Three of the contestants moved up from the junior division as I had. Luckily, they all placed lower than I did last year. I didn't want to have any more competition.

The ten-minute buzzer sounded. I started to stretch. A few waited around talking; that was a crucial mistake. With my luck, I would get a charlie horse or something. The one-minute buzzer went off. We all took our running positions. My pulse raced. Good, I would need the adrenaline. I channeled the adrenaline into my feet and focused on the part of the track I could see.

The sun was bright and hot. The minimal breeze would not be enough once I started running. I braced myself for the gunshot. A bald man held the gun in the air. The sun sparkled off his head. I didn't have time to smile. The gun went off, and my legs leaped forward along with the others. I pushed every ounce of my focus on following the path. If I missed a marker or a tree branch, I would be lucky to finish at all. I didn't have time for a sprained ankle or a fall.

[Pace yourself Jon.] Rose reminded me.

I slowed down a little. Half a mile out of the way. It's not a sprint, I told myself. I jumped over a fallen log. A few minutes later, I ducked to avoid hitting a limb with my head. A concussion wouldn't help me now. One mile down, one to go. I heard several other runners keeping my pace. I continued running as I wiped the sweat off my forehead.

The desire to rush into a sprint was almost too much, but Rose was right. It was better to keep the same pace all the way through the race. I jumped over another log. And dodged a few more trees.

The sounds of feet were dulling as I reached the one and half mile marker. I avoided a huge rock. If I had more time, it would have been fun to explore the area. Rose would love it. She didn't like wandering off the path this far in, but it was marked, I reasoned. One and three quarters of a mile. I was almost there. I could smell the fuel from the Vaktows in the air.

Suddenly, I broke through the forest and saw the crowds held at bay by ropes. I was the second one out of the forest by a few seconds. Jasmine was first. I grinned. At least she was blood. The cheers erupted.

I rushed to my designated Vaktow. This was my chance to pull ahead. The next half of the race would be my weakest. Cheers screamed again. Someone else must have made it through the trees. I grabbed my water bottle and downed half a liter in a few gulps. I set it aside and picked up a diagnostic tool.

I checked the exhaust, and the motor; when I got to the wiring, I saw the problem. The control panel was disconnected. I quickly connected seven wires and put everything back in place. As I screwed in the last screw to the control panel, I remembered what Jaz had said.

Something slid into place. There were two problems last year, but one was a lot more subtle. Does the Vaktow have fuel? Everything else is checked out okay. I quickly checked the fuel gauge. It was almost empty.

The farthest I would get without adding fuel would be a mile. The swim track was three miles from here down a river. I filled it up and left in the Vaktow for the swim portion. I was the first one to leave. It didn't take long to get to the river. I tore off my shirt to kill a few seconds off my swim time. My shoes were off in the next second.

I flew into the river. The lukewarm water cooled down my hot skin. I heard another Vaktow land. I propelled my body forward as fast as I could. It was only a half a mile swim. Another Vaktow landed. Crap!

I kicked as hard as I could and moved my arms in a systematic motion. It wasn't as fluid as some of the other swimmers, but I was doing okay. I felt the thoughts of another person coming up behind me on my left. I couldn't swim any faster, so I kept pace.

I could see the finish line up ahead; it wouldn't be long until I was there. I couldn't get a clear handle on the thoughts of the swimmer on my left. We were swimming neck in neck and to look would mean I'd lose my concentration and the lead. That meant one thing, royalty. It had to be Jaz. I knew Joe's thought pattern when I was this close, even if I couldn't read his mind.

[Jaz, what are you doing?] I asked.

[I told you I'd see you at the finish line.] She answered.

[How close is Joe?] I couldn't help asking. Fifteen more

seconds and I would be out of the water.

[Not sure, but he is in the river.] Jasmine responded.

I pulled myself out of the water; a kid threw me a towel as I raced into the big white building. I wiped my hands and face off as I ran. A man stood there holding out a packet and a pencil. I grabbed them out of his hands and murmured a thanks.

Joe came in next and sat in a chair next to me. He had been closer than I thought. Focus Jon! You can do this! I stumbled to open the packet before Joe did. Jaz came in before I could read the first question. This was Joe's best portion of the Zanxtear Race, but I made it this far. So far, I am in first. Breathe, you can do this, you can…

1. If a Ratillian kidnaps you, what is the best possible way to be rescued?

Are they serious! I wrote down one word, Jahni, and moved on to the next question. It was multiple choice. The third was true and false. The fourth was an in depth question on how to prevent a war between two kingdoms. It listed several facts. I did my best and hurried through each question. As each minute ticked away, new people entered the room and took the packet handed to them.

I thought about Paul's advice. Well, I have found Joe, and I stayed ahead of him, for the most part. I finished question nine and started reading the tenth question. Joe stood up and quickly took the packet to the grader. I finished the last question and got up when Jasmine slid behind Joe and handed her packet forward. I put mine beside Jasmine's. She beat me! I was so close, about a minute close.

The grader nodded her head. "Eight out of ten."

Joe wasn't happy that he missed two. He was ushered out of the building and cheers rushed. Ugg! What if I missed one? Oh no! I turned to see the door close behind him. The woman was grading Jaz's.

Anticipation flew through my body, starting in my toes and rushing to my head. I felt like I could do the whole race over again. The lady nodded. I looked over Jasmine's shoulder to see a nine out of ten. Wow! If only I was that lucky, but I knew it was more than luck. Jaz was incredibly intelligent. Jasmine flashed me a smile that said told ya.

She graded mine quickly. As she flashed through each question, I started feeling numb. You only go through questions that fast when they're wrong, right? I gulped. She turned the packet around so I could see the grade, seven out of ten.

"Good enough for third." She smiled.

There were a few groans.

Yes! I made it. It took a second for the numbness to wear off. Someone came up behind me. I exited out the door with my packet. The cheers got louder when I opened the door and lifted up the packet with a seven on it.

A few guards drug me by the elbows over to the winners' circle. One blocked my front and one followed. Joe's grin was more of a smirk. Jasmine's was much more genuine. Jaz wrapped her arms around me in an excited hug.

"Congrats Jon!" She pulled back.

"You too!" I beamed. [I actually took third!]

[And I took first.] Joe's voice thumped into my head.

Ugg. He beat me. "Good job Sloane." I tried to get one more jab in, but Joe only smirked in response. It faded quickly into a smile.

"You too!" Joe shook my hand and wrapped his other hand around me in a guy hug.

"You did good." Jahni slipped in and gave Sloane her own personal congratulations, so I searched the crowds.

"You placed!" Rose squealed.

I beamed. "Surprised?"

"I wasn't sure." Rose confessed.

[Neither was I.] She laughed, and I did too.

Paul pushed through the crowd. He held out his hand to me and I shook it. "You know, you only made third because of this arm." He winked at me.

I laughed. "You're probably right." I admitted.

The man at the speaker began. "This year's first place

winner is King Joseph Smeltzer Sloane of Zalnorel; second place goes to the beautiful Jasmine Andrea Lopez Princess of Landryn, and third place goes to our newcomer Jon Robert Julian Prince of Zalnorel. He shows a lot of promise for the future. King Joseph and Princess Jasmine may want to watch out next year." The crowd cheered. Joe took his place in the middle on the winner's block.

We lined up with Joe in the middle, and Jasmine and I stood on either side. When they placed the gigantic trophy in his hands, the crowd screamed. They placed a smaller trophy in Jasmine's hands. She held it up in the air and the crowd cheered again. I received a slightly smaller trophy and held it up in the air, and the crowd cheered for me too.

"Give it up for our winners!" The announcer cried.

The crowd went wild. My heart raced, and I beamed. I didn't realize how much I would love the crowd cheering for me, well us, I admitted to myself. It sent a surge of adrenaline through my body. I could get used to this!

Joe set the huge trophy down. He raised my hand, and Jaz's hand in the air. I didn't think the crowd could get any louder, but they did. Jahni and Rose looked so proud of us, and so did Dad. Cameras flashed repeatedly, as if they were scared they would miss something important.

Later that afternoon, Dad took all of us out to lunch,

including Uncle Adeam, Aunt Delphie, and Jasmine. For some reason, Jasmine's brother Merrick couldn't make it. We weren't close, so I didn't mind.

You could taste excitement in the air. We talked easily back and forth. Joe teased me a few times about barely placing and I told him I had him all the way to the test, just because I test badly... He laughed and so did everyone else.

6

I ran up the stairs, slammed the door, and fell into bed. Thank God that's over. I pulled off my shirt and threw it across the room. Placing my hands behind my head, I looked up at the ceiling.

[Some days were better when they were finished.] I thought to myself.

[You can't mean that.] Rose responded.

[I don't?] I asked in a thought that said she had to be kidding.

[You did great!] Rose cheered.

[I did, for moving up to that division.] I told her.

[Jon, you need to stop being a drama King.] Rose told me.

[And I'm the one that is dramatic?] I asked.

I heard her soft laughter echo through my thoughts. She hadn't meant any harm, and to be honest, I hadn't been offended. I shook it off and covered up with my blankets.

[Night Rose.] I told her.

[But you aren't going to sleep right now.] She protested.

[I'm in bed and covered.] I told her.

[But you are complaining about coming in third and escaping embarrassment.] Rose was in pillow talk mode.

[Rose.] I growled.

[I am just trying to help.] She told me.

[Well, you're getting worse at it.] I thought back.

[You did great.] Rose tried again.

[I did okay. Goodnight.] I thought back to her.

[Great.] She countered.

[Not horrible.] I threw back at her.

[You almost won.] Rose stated.

[I did, didn't I?] I thought back.

[See.] Her thoughts were happy.

[Whatever.] I thought her way.

[I love you too.] Rose cheered.

[I didn't say that.] I told her.

[But you do. Goodnight.] Rose was grinning in her room. I could feel it from here.

[Whatever.] I told her again, but this time I was smiling.

7

The sun came shining through the window. It took my mind a minute to focus on what day it was. Yesterday was the Zanxtear Race. The trophy on my desk called to me and I stared at it. I actually came in third! A surge of joy electrified my body.

The worry I had forgotten flooded in. I spent half the night considering ways to get to Mom. Rose, and I had studied up on the Drex as soon as we came home a few years ago.

The Drecians were somewhat sophisticated. Their ships were virtually undetectable, not necessarily faster. They didn't expect any *real* challenge, because their weaponry is more advanced. Everything is protected by a 29-symbol password.

The Martels were ready for all forms of attacks at all times. The last known rescue from Drex without inside help was more than three centuries ago. We ran into a handful of stories about people in Drex helping people escape.

Somewhere in the night, I finally fell asleep. I spent most of the night playing out scenarios in my head. I couldn't predict what it would be like when we actually made it to Drex.

The sky was lighter, hinting the sun would be up soon. This is the only chance I'll have to be alone. I made a split second decision to get out of the house quickly. Before Jahni could reason with me, Joe could guilt me, and Rose could follow me.

I did my best to keep my thoughts to myself. One thing about living here, you could tip toe all you wanted, but if your thoughts were running around like fifteen dogs chasing five cats and ten squirrels, someone will still catch you.

Within three minutes, I was dressed and out of the house with a sandwich in one hand and a cold drink in the other. Guards were posted at the gate entrance, so I went around the back of the house, now halfway through my breakfast.

There was a creek running through the property in the midst of a quarter mile of trees. Rose would be asleep for hours unless someone woke her. Jahni, on the other hand… I examined the sky with my mouthful; maybe fifteen minutes.

I liked being the first to see the sun. Usually, I was too lazy to wake-up before the sun, but there is something magical about being on the cold ground with the first rays hitting your face. The sandwich was gone, so I thrust the cup up, and cold liquid chilled my stomach. I sighed and leaned back. I need more times like these. The solitude was peaceful.

Jahni started dreaming. With this pregnancy, her dreams were getting weirder and weirder. I attempted to block her visions out of my head. This one was about mounds and mounds of food. I sighed in frustration. Jahni was making me hungry again. I wonder why she is so late waking up. I pulled myself off the ground and lunged for the cup.

"Time to face my doom." I stood up like a man and headed out to conquer this dilemma.

Joe was leaning against the house. Oh great! It's never a good sign when someone is waiting on you. I noted the sun's height. An hour had passed. Joe backed off the wall. I guarded myself. He had a hidden purpose. The question was, what?

"You're up early." He spoke smoothly.

I decided to suck it up and be a man. "So are you. " I kept my tone even. He nodded.

"I wanted to talk to you." His voice was too calm.

I can see that! I bit back. [I'm not blind.] I let slip. Crap! "What about?" I questioned.

Joe walked toward me slowly. His mouth held a straight line. His body was too rigid.

"Let me guess, you decided to stay." I couldn't help the sarcasm.

Joe nodded as if he had been caught. At least he looked a little guilty. He stopped in front of me.

"I knew you'd stay with her." I sighed.

He waited a moment before he replied. "You know you're up for this, don't you?"

I didn't say anything and looked at the ground.

"You got skill too, man." He jabbed me in the shoulder with a grin.

I smiled with him and jabbed his shoulder back. We traded a couple of jabs before Joe tucked my head under his arm and knuckled it. Then he pushed me away, laughing.

"I'll try." I told him.

"You'll succeed." He spoke seriously.

I nodded.

"Rose ready?" He asked.

I rolled my eyes. "She's been packed for two months." Joe chuckled.

"You about ready?" He messed up my hair.

[Maybe.]

"We're getting closer to the, sure Joe you are absolutely right I'm all over it."

"Yeah, when it's over." I sighed.

He punched my shoulder again. "Hey, none of that."

We headed back home. Rose was standing at the top of the stairs outside the front door. She dropped two duffle bags beside a third. She looked quite proud of herself.

"What's all this?" I was baffled. She was actually up and awake without being pried out of bed.

"Carl is going to take them to the ship for me." She beamed.

Carl was a handyman. He could repair anything and did a lot of the rearranging and lifting when it came to the heavy stuff. He has been working for my father for years. I gave her a dumb look.

"You finally decided to go." She said the statement as if I should understand. She shook her head in frustration.

[Jon, I've been waiting for you to be ready to go to MaCownia, so we can go find out where Mom is. I knew about Jahni a while ago and, like you, I couldn't see Joe leaving her. I have been waiting for you to embrace our adventure!] She glowed.

My dumb look wouldn't go away. "You've been waiting the past two months on me?" By now, I was at the top of the stairs with her. Joe excused himself and headed inside.

[Of course silly, I'm not going without you.] Rose declared with a smirk.

Carl came out, picked up the three duffle bags, and made his way down the steps. He was taking them to our ship.

"Thanks Carl." Rose smiled her sweetest smile.

"You're welcome Princess Rose." He blushed.

The next thing I knew, Rose took hold of my arm and drug me into the house.

[What are you doing?] I complained.

[Well, you might want to know what's going on.] Her thought was about the strategy.

[You're an angel!] I exclaimed.

[I know.] She bounced.

Rose knew I was dreading the planning part the most, and she had already taken care of it! Thank you Rose! I felt like singing, but that wouldn't be the prettiest sound to hear, so I let Rose lead me to a room downstairs.

Rose was bubbling over with happiness. "Basically, we're going to MaCownia and find Bill Aisle. Listen to his Intel, advice, and go to Drex. There we will find Mom and ditch the bad guys." She smiled.

[That easy?] I asked.

"Yep." Her head bobbed.

I couldn't help remembering, that's where Hálie lived.

"Dad gave us enough money/merchandise to afford a small planet." Rose informed me. "Come on, let's get your bag."

We walked upstairs. I had my bag packed in my closet. I went and grabbed it out.

"Salaranda packed us tons of food." Rose sat bouncing on my bed.

I shook my head and put the bag over my shoulder. [I guess I'm ready whenever.]

[Dad said to see him first.] I nodded my agreement.

[I think Dad is in his office.] Rose jumped up and pranced out the door.

I followed Rose downstairs and down the hallway to Dad's office. Several family pictures hung on the blue walls. Rose knocked on the door and opened the door without a response.

Dad looked up sadly. Rose walked over and sat on Dad's desk. I dropped down into a large comfy chair.

"Morning." I said.

"Yeah, I'm not happy with Shokten to say the least." I could feel Dad's blood boiling from here. "I would be leaving with you this moment if he hadn't threatened civil war." Dad closed his eyes.

"We could wait." Rose offered.

"No, I plan on joining you soon enough. I think I can talk him into holding off for a little while, so I can leave. I've tried to convince him to let Jahni and Joseph take over my responsibilities, but he won't have it. He says it must be me or no one." Dad cringed. "If you can find out what happened to Miranda, the sooner the better. I don't know how long Shokten will drag this out."

"Okay." Rose and I said together.

[Remember to stay in this time space flow.] Dad inserted.

I nodded. The monitors on the ship should indicate that immediately. Each planet has its own gravitational pull. As long as we stay in the space that lines up with our planet's gravitational pull, we will come home to the same people. If we spend too much time in a place, that has a significantly slower gravitational pull than our planet, Dad, Jahni, and Joe will age faster than Rose and I. In fact, we could come back with our niece or nephew older than we are. If we go the other way, Rose and I could come back older than our father. I didn't like that idea either.

[I will.] He knew from my Triz, that I took it seriously. "When do we leave?" I forced my tone even.

"In an hour." Rose said cheerfully.

An hour! I wanted to growl. What was she thinking?

"Well, everything is ready. I thought you might want to eat first, that's why we're waiting." She was bouncing with excitement and meant each word.

Waiting? An hour was waiting. I turned around and threw a hand in the air. "Food it is."

Jahni stifled a giggle. And I could feel Joe fighting a smile. Rose skipped beside me.

"I love you, Jon." Jahni smiled. "You know what?"

"What?" I asked. She gave me a hug, and I hugged her back tight.

She looked up at me with teasing eyes. "You're my favorite brother."

"I'm your only brother." I grumbled.

"Touché." Joe commented.

I glared at him. Jahni laughed. Rose was giggling.

Her look turned serious. "Be safe."

"I will." I promised.

[Watch out for Rose.] She directed. I nodded.

A vow to protect Rose, I took seriously. I'd give my life for her. I had my issues, and probably should be less sarcastic, but my sister and best friend is more precious than any of that. She had faith in me when no one else did. But most of all, I can be the biggest jerk in the whole galaxy, a selfish jerk, and she still wants me around.

[Don't leave her alone for a second in MaCownia.] Jahni's thought struck a chord.

She didn't have to mention our last trip, or what would have happened if Joe hadn't had enough money to keep her from those…my thoughts turned malicious when I thought of what those beasts could have done to Jahni or her cellmate Hálie. My Blood was boiling.

[Never.] I vowed to Jahni.

"Be safe." She reminded.

"Love you Jahni." I planned to be safe, but if it ever came down to my life for Rose's, my life would be on the line in a heartbeat.

Jahni held Rose in a tight hug. Rose was still bouncy. "You're my favorite sister Rose."

Rose beamed. "I know." She giggled. "You're my favorite sister too!"

I rolled my eyes. They were dorks. But my heart swelled with love for them and my body ached in anticipation for the unknown.

Dad showed up out of nowhere and thrust me into a hug. [I love you son.] I didn't know what to say.

"Um yeah." I stuttered.

"Sorry I can't go with you, but I need to seal up this mess with Shokten. Adam should be in touch."

"Yeah. Sure." I responded. I didn't understand why he didn't just call him Adeam like the rest of us. "Okay, Rose."

I hated Jahni not coming. I didn't know what we'd do without Joe's diplomatic skills. And Dad had his own stubborn way of bringing us together.

I knew Dad wanted to come with us more than anything. The problem was Shokten had declared war on Zelle's 6th

Kingdom Jade. He refused to talk to anyone, but Dad. Apparently, Dad saved his life sometime before we were born and Shockten is too stubborn to listen to anyone else.

Rose passed a few more hugs away before running on board. I turned to follow.

"Hey Jon." I turned around at the sound of Joe's voice.

"Yeah?" I asked. He slung out his arm. I took it in a firm handshake.

"Wish I was going." He said.

Me too. I looked at Jahni, who stood a few paces behind him. "Take care of my sister."

"I always do." He grinned.

[I know.] "Later."

I rushed onto the ship before I thought too much about our last trip, or about Josiah making it possible for us to go. Instead, I took control of the ship and zoomed off towards MaCownia. At least this ship only needs one driver. Rose can drive as well as I can, but she usually lets me. She knows I enjoy it more than she does. She'd probably do okay in a Zanxtear Race, but she isn't into engines or competing professionally.

The ship would only hold ten people comfortably. There were four bedrooms. One had a large bed; the second had two sets of bunk beds. The others had two beds apiece.

"When are you going to get excited?" Rose tilted her

head adorably.

Never! "Maybe later Rose." I sulked.

"Jon, what's wrong?" I heard the way she heard me. She thought I sounded hurt.

I sighed. Joe and Jahni weren't here, so there wasn't any point in pretending. "I guess I am just feeling the stress."

She sighed too. "I know. You were dreaming about it non-stop before the Zanxtear Race."

Great! I forgot about that. "Did Jahni know?"

She bit her lip thoughtfully. "Sometimes yes, but I covered up most of them."

It was easier for royals to seal another's thoughts. Since we were twins, it worked even better. I knew Jahni; she tried not to pry into our thoughts unless she thought there was an extremely good reason. She only did it once that I remember.

"Good." I gave her a twisted smile.

"Oh, come on Jon. Cheer up!" She ordered. "This isn't going to be half as fun with you like this."

"Fine, I'll try!" I was exasperated.

"That's not trying." She rolled her eyes.

I wished there was something to concentrate on, so I could avoid her questions. What am I kidding myself? That isn't going to happen! Besides, I could put the ship on autopilot and go to sleep for the next hour, and nothing would happen. Sometimes it is a pain when everything is going smoothly.

"Hálie lives on MaCownia." I changed the subject.

"So?" Her tone took a sharp edge.

"Well, we haven't seen her in a while."

"Where is this going?" Her tone was less than pleased.

I peeked at her out of the side of my right eye. I didn't get why she got all defensive every time Hálie popped into my head. It was going to be an awful trip if we fought the whole way. Ugg!

"I want to go by." There, I said it.

"No." She snapped.

"Why not?" I exploded.

"We don't have the time." Her voice was serious.

"Since when?" I demanded. I spent the month getting ready for the Zanxtear Race and now we don't have time to make a quick stop for an hour or two! "What's your problem?" I cut.

"I don't have one."

"I am going to see Hálie." I said slowly and quietly.

She was cute. Why wouldn't I want to go see her? It has been three years, maybe she found someone else. Jealousy erupted with anger. I didn't need that right now. I threw out that idea and decided she was still single. The jealousy lifted.

She sighed. "Jon."

"What?"

"She is not good for you."

I looked at my sister. Was she serious? I noted her concern. She was serious! It wasn't as if I was in love with Hálie, nothing like Joe and Jahni.

"I will decide what's good for me." I growled back.

"Fine." She crossed her arms and leaned back in her seat.

I stared into space while she glared off to the right. Ugg. I wasn't mad, but she was. "I don't want to fight."

She peeked at me. Her mouth twitched. "I don't either." She frowned. "You still want to go see *that* girl?"

"Yes."

She sighed. "Okay."

8

Hálie's head lifted to see us coming. Her hands held a basket full of vegetables. Her blonde hair swayed with the wind. Her hair was longer than it was the last time I saw her. Her blue eyes sparkled in the sun. She quickly put the basket down and walked over to meet us.

"You came back!" She threw her arms around each of us.

"Of course we came back. We had to make sure you were alright." I told her.

"What are you doing here?" She asked.

"We are on a scavenger hunt." Rose beamed.

Rose's cheeks were bright and her smile contagious. I felt one slipping over my lips. I guess looking for a blue-haired man, finding Drex, and looking for our Mom can count as a scavenger hunt. Rose was always the optimist.

"I like scavenger hunts!" Hálie's excitement overflowed.

"It is a private scavenger hunt." Rose inserted carefully.

"Oh." She looked disappointed. "At least you can stay a few days." She cheered up.

"Actually." Rose glanced at me. "We have a previous engagement."

I felt sheepish. I hadn't been thinking about Bill Aisle.

"Oh, really?" She was unperturbed. "Who with? Maybe I can help you find them."

Rose's lip twitched. My sister obviously hadn't been prepared to deal with this unforeseen obstacle. It hadn't been her idea to stop. I was the genius who came up with it. In fact, I insisted.

"Just someone we ran into last time we were here." Hálie was harmless, but it is always a good idea to keep as much information as possible to yourself. 'Knowledge is power.'

"Well, maybe Aunt Gena will let you spend the night here?" She was hopeful.

I remembered the inn we stayed in the last time we were here. Aunt Gena's had to be better than that mold infested room.

"We'll pay you." I offered.

Hálie huffed and waved me off. "That's not necessary." She walked with us to her porch.

"We actually have rooms on our ship." Rose smiled, trying to get rid of Hálie.

"You don't want to stay in there when you can have fresh air." Hálie declared in disgust.

"Are you sure?" Rose tried to find a polite way to decline.

We were standing beside the door on the front porch.

"Yes, I just have to go ask Aunt Gena. You wait here." Hálie disappeared before Rose could come up with an excuse that Hálie would accept.

Hálie poked her head into the other room. "Aunt Gena." I heard a mumbled response, and she walked into the room. "Remember, I told you about my friends that rescued me, well can they spend the night?"

She came bouncing back. Her blonde hair danced off her shoulders with every step. "She said yes!" Hálie exclaimed.

"Oh, good." Rose muttered under her breath, piercing her eyes at me like daggers.

I shrugged my shoulders and pretended I didn't understand what she meant. Hálie was smiling from ear to ear, and I couldn't help smiling with her. It was going to be an interesting day.

9

"So you kids came back after all." Bill chuckled.

This time, his eyes were closer to mine. Rose had grown taller too.

"We came to take you up on your offer." I told him.

He eyed me. His tone held its own ground. His patch came off as mysterious and his good eye hinted danger. His blue hair over shadowed the black. He was still young enough to do some damage. He wore an open leather vest without sleeves. His muscles filled out the rest.

"Humph. So you have." He placed his hands on his hips, appearing judgmental. "Come."

He walked between me and Rose, running his shoulder into mine to let me know he was in charge. We both looked at him in surprise. Rose and I followed Bill Aisle away from the open street to a secluded table outside the inn. We ordered quickly.

"Well." His eyes fell on us dumbly. "Tell me about it."

"Huh?" I was completely oblivious.

He gave us a 'duh' look. He gestured with his hand. "For starters, you did what I told you last time and went home..." He prodded.

We nodded.

"And?" He asked.

Finally, I found my voice. "And we heard a storm was going to hit again and went home. It cleared up. So we came back."

He grunted. "It's never that simple. What happened to the others that came last time?"

[He doesn't know where we are from.] Rose reminded me.

[Or who we are.] I reminded her. A man like this was just as likely to help you as sell you for a ransom.

"Jahni and Joe are expecting." I told him.

His eyebrows went up and his eyes widened. "Really?"

Rose nodded. "That's why they decided not to come. They will be sorry they missed you."

He grunted. "I guess that makes sense. So you are going to Drex on your own." His voice was skeptical.

"Yes." I told him.

"What kind of ship do you got?" Bill asked.

"You'll help us?" Rose questioned.

"I said I would!" He stammered.

Success! I grinned. "How 'bout we show you?" I told him.

He nodded an okay. We paid for the meal and headed to the docking bay. I unlocked the shield by the thought activation sequence Joe had helped me set up. The thought password would only work for someone from Zelle. The shield had two password options: Jon Robert Julian, or Rose Madison Julian.

"You're planning on taking that!" Bill asked us.

"What's wrong with it?" I demanded.

"What's wrong with it?" He asked incredulously.

I nodded a yeah.

"It's too flashy. I thought you wanted to save your mother, not become a part of the museum!"

[Why hadn't I thought of that?] We can't take it to Drex. Bill Aisle was right. It screamed Zellian. It was the newest model and would be a *prize find* for anyone looking for new art in their exhibit.

"So what do you suggest?" I asked. He looked thoughtful and scraped his chin with his left hand.

"I have just the thing." He grinned wickedly.

[Of course you do.] I thought to Rose. She bit back a laugh.

10

Bill Aisle sauntered back proudly. I could almost see the dollar signs coming off of him. This was going to cost us ten times more than it was worth if Bill had anything to do with it. I steeled my presence, so I was less likely to be manipulated.

"Follow me." Bill turned around and walked back in the direction he had come.

The fumes in the air hung like continuous rain pelting my skin, making it hard to see a long distance away. We passed several shady looking characters, both male and female. I almost ran into Bill Aisle when he stopped abruptly.

[This is it?] I was appalled. [Can it make it to Drex?]

[I don't know.] Rose's face scrunched up in shock.

The ship was stained with black oil and flat out dirt. It needed to be washed. There was a dent on the front end and the top indicating it had been in a few collisions -possibly another ship or debris which would indicate a malfunctioning Debris Sifter. The Debris Sifter wouldn't take long to fix if the right parts were available.

I groaned inwardly. [This was the ship Bill Aisle found for us?]

Bill patted the beat-up ship. "It has character." He grunted as if he didn't believe it either.

I rolled my eyes.

"It... uh... just looks a little rough from... uh... hard living." Bill Aisle searched for words that would make this dinosaur look younger.

[How much more hard living can she take?] Rose asked.

I coughed to hide my laugh. He gave me a sharp look. I shrugged my shoulders as if to say what? He turned his attention back to the ship. He gave us a rough tour, pointing at closed doors. He led us straight to the control room without any detours. Other than a few junk boxes sitting around, it looked decent.

I crossed my arms. "I want to see the engine room."

He wasn't happy about it, but he left the room we followed. Here it is. He opened the door, but stayed in the hallway. He was hoping I wouldn't enter. I am not a fool. There were junk boxes piled in here too. What was this place, a storage unit?

I went straight to the Debris Sifter. Everything around it looked old, but the Debris Sifter looked much newer. It must have been replaced recently. That was good news.

I tapped my WC, Wrist Com, on. I had updated my

Magnesystem on my WC to recognize various ships outside our galaxy. I ran a scan. It beeped twice. It recognized the ship. A 3D image projected out of my Com and scanned over each wire on the ship.

"What's that?" Bill was curious.

"A Magnesystem." I watched the images intently. So far, everything was in working condition.

"What is it doing?" Bill stepped into the room.

"Analyzing the ship's ability to fly, land, and length of said abilities. If anything needs fixed, it should tell me immediately." I watched the red dots fly along the wires, each one lighting up green when the wire was confirmed as efficient for transportation purposes.

I spent an hour looking everything over; before I concluded, the ship would hold together. We would need two back up energy sources though. This one was a bit low. It needed a few new filters too. It should hold out for fifty more galaxies. Drex was approximately nine galaxies away. I thought about taking it home, then threw the idea away. It would be better to sell it when we come back here for our ship.

"So what do you think?" Bill Aisle throughout the question, hoping I was still a willing buyer.

"How much?" I asked.

Bill grinned back. He knew I was about to buy it. He

started guesstimating how much it was worth and how much he could get out of it if someone else were to buy it.

"You're not going to overcharge us." I stared him down.

"Wouldn't think of it." He responded.

"Of course you wouldn't." Rose said sweetly. [Good going Jon!] She cheered.

We finally rested on a fair number. Dad had given us enough money to buy a small planet if need be. We gave him the money with plenty to spare.

He threw me the control crystal. "Pleasure doing business with you." He gloated.

[I bet.] I thought.

[Just smile and wave.] Her smile was fake.

We watched Bill Aisle walk away happily. We left our pile of ship bones to get our stuff off of our much nicer, newer ship. Somehow, this seemed upside down. I exhaled. It was such a shame to leave this here, and leave in our newly acquired wreck.

"I know, Jon." Rose had put down one of her bags to pat me on the back.

"Yeah." I turned away from the beauty.

With a thought, the ship cloaked itself and was invisible to the naked eye.

11

[Did you hear that?] My sister asked.

I didn't have any idea what she was talking about. I listened. The ship creaked like it had been doing for the last few hours. Other than that, I heard nothing.

[Rose I don't hear...] Bang. [What was that?] I stood up.

[I don't know, but I heard it before. I think it's over there.] She pointed beside the door.

Behind that wall was the engine room. I glanced at the screen and indicated she took over. I scanned the room and picked up a three-foot bar out of one of the junk boxes. I curled my fingers around an end and tested the weight.

I cautiously moved toward the door. I heard the sound again. It was definitely coming from the engine room. I opened the door to the hallway and peeked around the corner. I didn't see anyone or anything out of the ordinary, so I moved my body around the frame.

I opened the door just enough to see inside. I didn't see anyone, but I saw a nut roll across the floor. I closed my eyes in a quick prayer before I flung the door open to enter the room. My eyes followed the general direction the nut had come from. I saw a locker door open an inch. I took three long strides and threw open the door with my trusty bar clenched in my other fist.

Brown hair hovered inside the locker. Then a child's face looked up at me. It was a boy. He stared up into my face with fear.

"Hey kid, what are you doing in there?" My clenched fist loosened as I crossed my arms, bar still in hand. He didn't say anything.

[Jon?] Rose asked.

[I found him.] I told her.

[Him?] She was curious.

[Yeah, some kid has been hiding in the engine room.] Disgust rang through my thoughts.

"Jon?" Rose was standing by in the doorframe.

I turned to look at her. I felt her send a Triz of surprise, and then a body ran into my left side and ran past me. I backed up slightly, not expecting him to run.

"Oh, no you don't." I growled and charged at him.

Rose blocked the doorway. He couldn't get around her. I let the bar drop to the ground and grabbed him around the waist. He started kicking. I held his arms down. He bent his head to bite my hands, but his teeth were too far away.

"What is wrong with you?" I yelled at him. He paused for a second, surprised at my tone.

"Nothing is wrong with me!" He yelled back just as loud.

This kid was getting on my nerves. "Rose, get some rope!"

"From where?" She asked.

"I don't know! Just get some!" I yelled in frustration. I was ready to throw this kid back into the locker and stand in front of it to block him in.

She looked around the room frantically. He tried to jab his head back into me, but couldn't get enough leverage to do any damage. The kid was kicking again.

"Oww!" I screamed in pain. He kicked me in the shin. I held my legs together. His mouth dove for my hand again, but he still couldn't reach them.

"Listen kid! Stop it! We are in the middle of space. Where are you going to go?" I hissed in his ear. He stopped for a moment and then started struggling again. Rose finally found an old rope.

"Here." Rose took hold of one of the kid's wrists.

"I can handle his arms, get his legs." I told her in frustration.

She let go of his wrist. She tied a quick loop and tossed it over a shaking foot. She managed to get his legs tied without suffering.

"You." He huffed, "cannot do..." He struggled to get out of the ropes and failed. "...this to me!"

"Wanna bet!" I dared. He gave up trying to kick free. The ropes had done their job.

"Do you know what my father will do to you and your family when he finds out you have restrained me?" He spoke calmly.

"Quite indignant for a kid." I muttered. If he wanted to be a brat, I would treat him like a brat. I shook him a little.

Rose gave me a light warning look. I held the kid tightly in place. He was still. His involuntary Triz were searching for a new strategy. What was going on with him? I looked over at Rose again. Her face was thoughtful.

"What is your name?" Her voice was soft.

He spat. "My father will."

"Your father isn't here!" I cut him off.

A Triz of sorrow escaped. Then I was right. We wouldn't have some sort of mutiny on our hands. So far, good cop, bad cop was going well. Rose had her part down to a tee. I'm not too bad at playing a bad cop, either.

[The kid is here all alone. Wonder where his Dad actually is?] I asked Rose.

[I don't know.] Her thought was sad. She always cared

too much about the injured, whether it was their spirits or bodies. [What are we going to do with him?]

Ugg! [We are too far into space to turn back.]

[You're right. But we can't keep him tied up the whole time, can we?] Her thought was gentle.

The thought wasn't appealing, but Rose was probably right. We have a few more days ahead of us; it wouldn't be right to have him tied up that long.

[What about one of the extra rooms? We could leave him in there and lock the door.] I suggested.

[Maybe.] She said slowly. "Honey, what is your name?" She cooed tenderly.

He gulped. "Xandermalion Avadartanrisan."

Huh? Wow, and I thought Jahni had a mouthful of a name! "So Zander, why are you here, on this ship?"

"I'm thirsty!" He complained.

I rolled my eyes. "Sure you are." I soaked my words in sarcasm.

"And hungry too!" He whined.

"I'll get him something." Rose sighed.

"Uh…Who is driving?" I asked.

"It's on auto-pilot, but I will check it before I grab the food." She left the room. [It's fine.]

"I guess it's me and you, kid." I huffed at him. I wish

there was somewhere I could put him, but with all these junk piles, he could easily escape and cut himself loose.

"I have a name." He pouted.

"Sure you do, Zander." I didn't care.

"No, it's Xandermalion Avadartanrisan." He insisted.

"Well, I am going to call you Zander; it's much simpler for a kid. You can be the other name when you grow up." Ugg kids! When did I sign up to be a babysitter?

"You are going to regret it when my father comes." He protested.

"Yeah, and when is that? Next month, next year?" I mocked.

He let off another unintentional sad Trizmente. I felt sorry about the comment. I didn't mean to hurt the kid's feelings, but I wasn't about to let him know that.

"Look Zander, we're stuck with you at least until we reach the next planet and then you can tell your father where you're at. Sound alright?"

"When we arrive on Drex, right?" He sounded hopeful.

My body stiffened. No one was supposed to know we were going to Drex. How did Zander know?

[Rose, we have a problem. This kid knows we are going to Drex.] I informed her. I didn't like where this was going. My jaw clenched.

87

"You *are* going there?" His words were eager.

"Why would anyone want to go to Drex?" My voice came out stiff and fake.

"But...but..." His hope changed into confusion.

"But what?" How could he know? Who is he?

"I heard that man say you were going there when I was hiding." Zander insisted.

Bill Aisle! Great! I fumed. We could have just dropped him off and some random planet with enough money to get him home, but now...I don't know. If Bill had kept his mouth shut when we switched ships...but he didn't.

[Bring him over to the control room.] Rose instructed.

"Come on." I heaved him through the door.

"Hey!" He complained. "Where are you taking me?"

He wouldn't stop complaining the whole way to the control room, and it was a long hallway. I stuffed him into a chair. He glared at me. His hands were still free.

"You think you can sit there, or should I tie up your hands too?" He crossed his arms. Man did that look familiar.

"I can handle it." He grumbled.

"Good." [I didn't know how much longer I could have restrained him. My arms were getting tired.] Rose laughed.

"What's so funny?" The boy asked us.

I took a better look at him. He was thin. His clothes were

expensive. Maybe his father was something to actually consider. He may be a diplomat. Oh, Joe and Jahni would love to explain this to the neighboring planets. [I can see the headlines now. Prince of Zelle kidnaps boy.]

Rose heard my thoughts. [You're not going to like this, but we will have to deal with the father. Jahni and Joe are too far away. We are in charge of diplomacy.]

My jaw loosened. [No!]

[Yeah.] She handed the boy a drink and a sandwich. After he ate a few bites, she asked, "Do you want to tell us how you got here?"

"No." He took another drink.

I bent down and glared into his eyes. "Let me rephrase the question. Do you want to tell us what is going on, or do you want us to throw you into a cargo box, nail down the lid, and drop you off on the next planet in the middle of a field?"

Zander gulped. "You would not do that. Would you?"

"She wouldn't. But I would." He believed me.

I didn't mention I would probably come back for him after he had a few hours to think. The boy twitched. Hopefully, he was scared enough to talk. We needed some answers, especially if we had some diplomat's son.

"You will not do that if I tell you?" His voice quivered.

Rose sent a glare my way for scaring Zander. In my

defense, it was the only way I could think of to get him to talk. He sat his half-eaten sandwich down. His drink tilted in his hand.

"No, of course not." Rose soothed, rubbing his head tenderly like a mother would her crying child. "Now, tell us what brought you here."

The boy craned his head upward to meet my gaze. He swallowed hard and looked down.

"Well, my father was on a…" He paused, "lucrative business trip."

[Did he just say lucrative?] My brow wrinkled. She nodded. What kind of kid was this?

"I snuck off our ship when we were on MaCownia to explore. They did not know I was gone. I have been looking for a way home ever since."

[Home! And he wants to go to Drex. Rose, we have a real problem on our hands.] I was horrified. She agreed.

"How long ago was this?" She asked kindly.

"A few weeks." He shrugged his shoulders.

"Any chance they will go back to MaCownia to look for you?" Her voice was gentle.

"I doubt it. They think I am in my room with the hologram tutor."

"What about meal time?" I asked. "Wouldn't they notice you are missing?"

He shook his head. "My room has a machine that makes my food for me. No one will come looking for me until they arrive back home. I'm tired." He complained.

[Can you handle him?] I asked, already heading to the door.

[Yeah, I should be fine.] She assured me.

I left the room as he asked. "Where is he going?"

I grumbled again, wondering why I let Bill Aisle talk me into buying this piece of junk. The staircases weren't wide enough. At least I didn't have to worry about hitting my head. The ship only had three floors, including the cargo bay.

I traveled down the stairs where I quickly saw a problem, no keys to lock the doors from the outside. I didn't trust the boy enough to go to sleep with him in the other room. I searched madly through several boxes in the hallway outside of our rooms. I stuffed a few nails and screws in my pocket as I came to them. I also stuffed a screwdriver and a hammer into my back pocket.

I opened up the door to my room and dumped out the first box I saw. It didn't have anything too useful; I thought as I scrambled to step over the rolling flashlight, batteries, nail clippers, tape, and faded books. I flung open the top dresser draw and then the next. When I opened the last drawer, I found a rope, some papers, and a padlock.

"Thank you, God!" I proclaimed to my trashed room. I

sloshed through the junk into the dimly lit hallway.

I walked over to the spare bedroom. I looked around. I dropped the padlock on the bed, stacked one box on top of another, and brought it into the hallway. I saw a smaller door that might be a closet. I took five long strides over to open the door. It was a closet, but the top two shelves were full of sheets and other clothes. I set the two boxes on the floor. There was room for two more boxes.

I went back to Zander's new room. One more box was in the corner. I picked it up and moved it to the dresser. I emptied the contents into the box, filling it to the top. I carried it to the closet and stacked it on the others.

I groaned as I remembered I hadn't checked his closet. I went to my room and grabbed the empty box I had dumped over earlier. This room was getting pretty bad, so I opened my closet, which was surprisingly empty, and kicked in everything that was close inside and closed the door.

There, much better. I have a pathway out now. I closed my bedroom door too. When Rose sees it, she will probably say I'm living like an animal or something.

In his closet, I found a few hangers. I didn't trust him with those, so they went into the box along with an umbrella, a harmonica, some bolts, and a pair of scissors. I scooped up the box, forced it to fit on top of the others, and closed the closet in the hallway before it all exploded everywhere.

Now for the padlock. I grabbed the package off the bed. That little brat wasn't going anywhere without supervision. I was proud of myself.

[What's taking so long?] Rose wanted to know.

[I'm almost done.] I promised.

She huffed, but returned to entertaining Zander.

I pulled out a knife from my pocket to undo the lock package. I folded the knife and slid the two keys safely away in my pocket. It didn't take long to install the padlock on the outside of his door. It should be out of his reach. The padlock was at my shoulder level.

I scanned his room again. I didn't see anything he could use as a weapon, or a means of escape. I rushed up the narrow staircase. It was a good thing I wasn't claustrophobic.

When I entered the control room, Rose and Zander were chattering away. Zander saw me out of the corner of his eye and turned his head.

"What took you so long?" He demanded.

I didn't like his tone. [I am in line for the throne, not that I want it. But that isn't the point. This brat had no right to demand anything from me. He was the one who stowed away on my ship.]

[Our ship.] Rose corrected.

[You know what I mean.] "It's none of your business." I informed him severely.

I took a few long strides until I was standing beside Rose. I stared him down. His jaw was slack, as if no one had talked to him like that before. Diplomat's son—right—I had forgotten.

[When the day comes, a Prince can't tell off a diplomat's kid I'm abdicating whatever rights I have. My sisters can handle them better anyway.] I hadn't made it to seething yet, but I was getting more angry as the seconds ticked by.

[You're handling it too.] Rose encouraged.

I turned my head sharply to meet Rose's gaze. I was surprised to see approval. What was the big deal? I was just being me.

[Funny. I didn't have any trouble getting answers after you left. He thinks I'm the good guy.] Rose grinned.

[Traitor.] I joked.

[I prefer spy.] She smiled. "It's about time for bed." She soaked him with sweetness.

I crossed my arms and threw in a scowl for effect. He looked at me warily.

As she walked him down the staircase, I heard him say. "He will not really lock me in a box and leave me in a field, will he?"

I bit back my laugh while I scanned the control panel.

Everything looked in order. I raced down the stairs. I heard her talking to him outside his room and leaned beside the door.

[Be there in a minute.] Rose had sensed I was waiting. I heard her finish up with a prayer and escaped out the door.

[He looks so sweet.] She cooed.

[Looks are deceiving.] My shin was a little bruised from earlier.

As soon as the door closed, I grinned mischievously, put the lock on the door, and locked it. I tossed her one of the extra keys.

She rolled her eyes. [I don't think he is planning on going anywhere.]

[You weren't the one getting kicked a while ago.] I argued.

[Come on.] She led the way to the control room. She plopped down in her chair. I sat carefully in mine. "You won't believe what he told me."

I already didn't like where this was going. What could he have said to Rose? I had been so focused that I had shut Rose out of my thoughts while I was clearing Zander a room.

"He is from Drex." Rose leaned forward.

"We knew that already." I was perturbed.

She continued. "I think his father is a Martel."

My eyes widened. "We have a Martel's son here?"

Zander hadn't been exaggerating. The Martels were equivalent to a king—Colonels. You didn't automatically become a Martel. You had to earn it. But if your father or mother had been a Martel. You were in line to take the position after they passed or gave it to you. Martels were in charge of various space bases and portions of Drex.

She followed my thoughts. "Don't worry about it Jon."

Don't worry about it! I haven't begun to worry! If this Martel declared war on us, the other Martels would join in. Zelle could be destroyed, all because I locked a boy in a room and threatened him.

"Jon." She cautioned.

I focused on Rose; it was safer that way. My mind didn't need to think about the devastation that could be done to Zelle. For all I knew, the Drecians had the power to obliterate Zelle into nothing but rock strewn across the galaxy.

"I think we did the right thing. He has never been told off before you. I believe it was good for him." Rose was thoughtful.

[Huh?] Her words didn't add up with the images in my head.

"I think we should get to know Zander and let him get to know us. I'm sure this will work out in our favor." Rose was using her convincing tone. My sister was beautiful, sweet, charming, and knew how to turn almost any situation her way.

"Rose, what are you planning?" My voice was careful, as if I was sneaking up on an alligator.

"I'm not sure yet, but." She paused. "It'll work out. Let's pray Jon."

I nodded an okay. God could take care of this mess; I mean, he took care of Jahni, so he can take care of us too. We bowed our heads.

Rose's voice came through. [God, you have a plan for us, even one for Zander. Please lead us. God to do your will in our lives. Find our mother and safely return us home. Take our worry and show us what to do. And God, please help get us to get Zander to his home safely too, while protecting Zelle. Amen.]

I looked up. "Do you want the first shift or second?"

"I better take first, you wake up easier." She grinned.

I smiled. "Night Rose. Love ya."

"Love ya too. Remember to let Zander out in the morning." She smiled.

I made a face. "Okay."

She laughed. I went quietly down the steps. As I passed Zander's room, I listened to his thoughts. All I could hear were lucid mutterings. It was enough that I knew he was half-asleep.

I walked over to my room and shut the door. The room was still trashed. The magic fairies forgot to stop by and clean my room. Yeah right, like there really are magic fairies. I opened

97

up the closet door and shooed some more junk in. This is my version of cleaning. I stripped down to my boxers and slid into bed.

I was too tired to dream, or stay up pondering on which strategies will work in the future. I was just not asleep and then asleep.

12

I heard giggles. My brain attempted to register where they were and whom they came from. Slowly, I came back to Reality. I shook my head and ran my fingers through my hair.

I pulled some clothes out of my duffle bag and pulled them on. In one of the smaller pockets of my duffle bag, I found a comb. I started sliding it through my hair as the door closed.

The laughter was falling down the stairs and bouncing off the metal. I took the stairs two at a time. I flung open the control room door.

"Good morning!" She smiled, but her eyes were tired from being up all night. The giggles stopped, and I found an extra set of eyes staring back at me.

[Why didn't you wake me?] I asked.

[Not a problem. We've had fun.] Her thoughts were getting slower. She was ready for sleep.

She giggled. I used my ability as the Prince of Zelle and I saw the way my eye quirked looked at her. I found myself smiling.

[Did I miss something?] The boy was puzzled.

I sobered up. And graced him a once over. He stiffened. I crossed my arms, attempting a foreboding look with the added scowl. He gulped hard, so it worked.

[You might want to make friends today.] Rose suggested.

My lip twitched. [Maybe, but you need some sleep.]

[He should be good 'til lunch.] She informed me.

[See you in five.] I responded.

[Try nine or ten hours.] She stood up.

I made a face, and she laughed. Zander appeared even more confused. He looked back and forth between us repeatedly.

"Um…Zander." His eyes poured into hers as if she was his refuge. "I need to get some sleep."

"No." He whimpered. She placed a kiss on top of his head.

"Yes." She stumbled toward the door. "See you in nine hours."

Zander looked at me and I looked back at him too. Maybe Rose was right. I needed to make a friend, if only for the kid's sake. I glanced at the monitors. Everything looked good, which I found boring. When everything is clear space for hours on end, there isn't anything to do.

"You eat?" I asked.

He nodded.

I looked around the room and saw a leftover plate already made. Rose thinks of everything. I sat down, legs stretched wide-open. I bowed my head and whispered a quick thank you to God. When I looked up, I found two brown eyes curiously watching my every move. I started eating. He didn't say anything. I finished and threw away the disposable plate.

I looked at the monitors. Nothing had changed. I looked at Zander. Now, what was I going to do?

"How old are you?" I asked.

[Nine. I'm not going to tell you!] He thought.

I wonder if that is how she found out her information.

"Can you count?" I went with a second question.

"Of course I can count." He was indignant.

"Good."

"Huh." The boy seemed to be confused a lot.

I rolled my eyes. "Come on." Reluctantly, he followed.

I went into my room and fumbled around until I found two decks of cards. I zipped it up while Zander watched intently. I kicked some junk away until I spotted a pen. I pulled a blank piece of paper out of the wreck. I shoved the door closed.

Zander stood there, dumbfounded. I turned to face him. "You just going to stand there?" He shook his head no and trailed me step for step.

If this is what little brothers are like, I'm glad Rose and I are the last ones. I pulled a cart over for a makeshift table and put the junk on the floor. Zander hadn't stopped staring.

"What's wrong with you?" I demanded.

"Nothing." He gulped.

I frowned, opened the two decks, and began to shuffle. He gawked in awe.

"What?" I asked him.

"How did you do that?" He asked in amazement.

"Do what?" My brows furrowed.

"That!" He pointed at the cards I was shuffling.

"The bridge?" I was puzzled.

"I guess." He sighed. "How?"

Zander gazed at me, eager to learn my trick. I gave him half the cards. I split the ones in my hands in half slowly. He fumbled and split his deck too.

"Now what?" His voice was eager.

I placed each half in a hard and grasped the top of the narrow side with my thumbs and the backs with my fingertips. He attempted to do the same, but one of the decks scattered across the cart and the floor. He scrambled to pick them up. I continued shuffling.

Once he had them all gathered again, I took my previous position and showed him the bridge. He tried and missed the pile altogether. He tried again, and some shuffled, but they ricocheted off in such a way it was against the grain and not the smooth feather like touch when the cards swiveled through my hands. He concentrated really hard, but no bridge. After five or so minutes, I was bored.

"Hey let's play the game, the rest takes practice." I took his piles and quickly melted them into the cards in my hand. I dealt him, me, him, me, him, me, and flipped the next card over.

"What are we playing?" Zander was eager to learn.

A game. What does it look like? "3-13." I said instead.

"What's that?" He was overly curious.

A game! Why so many questions? "Have you ever played 500 rummy?"

"No, what's that?"

This kid was useless. He couldn't even play 500 rummy! I exhaled and looked at the clock. I had eight and half more hours with him. I guess he's learning today.

"We'll play open-handed until you get it." I tried not to roll my eyes. Rose and Jahni were the teachers, not me.

"Okay?" He looked skeptical.

I laid my card hand flat in front of me so he could see my cards. And then I flipped his cards over, so I could see them. I wrote our names on the paper.

"The goal is to get the least amount of points for the whole

103

game. In the first round, I dealt three cards and threes are wild. In the next round, you'll deal four cards and fours will be wild. Then I'll deal five cards and fives will be wild. All the way up to kings. You want to make a lay like 7♥'s 7♦'s 7♠'s. Since there are two decks, you could have two 7♥'s and the third 7 for a lay. The same goes with jacks, 10's, aces, whatever."

He nodded again.

"For other lays you need the same suit. If you have 2, 3, 4 and want to lay them down, they all have to be clubs, or spades, or hearts, or diamonds. It could be 5, 6, 7, 8 instead. A wild card can substitute any card. So if you have a three this round and want to use it as a king or a two, you can. You got it?"

He gave me a blank stare.

"Look, let's just play." I grumbled.

He looked at the cards as if they were about to attack him.

"Draw." I pointed to the cards in between us.

He obeyed and placed it beside the other three cards.

"Now what?"

He had 10♠, 4♣, a 3, 2♦.

"The ten doesn't go with anything and it's the most points, so you want to discard it." I tapped the middle of the cart.

He put the card there. I drew a Jack of diamonds and frowned. That wouldn't do me any good, so I put it in the discard pile.

He nervously grabbed a card. Five of hearts. He held it up for me to see.

"Does it go with anything?" I asked him.

"No."

"Is it lower than your other cards?"

"No."

"Then you don't want it." I replied offhandedly.

He placed it in the discard pile. This time I pulled out a seven of clubs. If it'd been hearts, I would be making a lay and be out. I threw it away. He drew a six of clubs and started to throw it in the discard pile.

"Hey what are you doing?" I pointed at the four.

"But there isn't a five." He insisted.

I picked up the three and sandwiched it in the middle. "There you have a lay."

He grinned.

"Now discard the two." I instructed him.

He did. I drew my final card. It was a three of diamonds. I grinned. "I'm out too. We both get zero points."

Zander looked confused.

"Remember, no points are good." I reminded him.

After a few open handed rounds, he got the hang of it and remembered not to discard wilds. At least for the most part anyway. Two games and three hours later, the ship was still sailing smoothly. I stood up and stretched. "New game."

13

"Will she ever wake up?" Zander asked.

I had been thinking the same thing. I ran out of ideas to entertain him an hour ago. We had played four different card games, ate too much junk food, and *he* gave me a tour of the ship, telling me the best places to hide. I mentally saved them for later. This kid would run. Maybe not now, but eventually, especially if he ditched his father. It wasn't easy to ditch a Martel. They were known as excellent trackers with state-of-the-art weaponry.

We finally ended up in the hallway where our rooms were.

"So, what do you want to do now?" I asked.

"We could clean your room." He sounded excited.

I gave him a look that screamed, you're crazy! He took a step back. Oh great, I scared him again and I'm stuck with this kid for at least two more hours.

"What's wrong with my room?" I protested. He gave me a look of appalled disgust.

Now a nine-year-old is telling me I should pick up after

myself. I strode across the hall and flung open his room to prove my point. My jaw had a hard time staying up. Zander's bed was made. Dust had been wiped away. It looked eight times better than my quick declutter job yesterday. Well, that defense won't work. I can't use his room as an example. I turned my head to look at him while my hand still held the door open.

A string of thoughts raced through his head about his father finding his room a mess, unacceptable, tears, and hiding. He looked down at the ground.

"I'm used to it like that at home." His voice was on the edge of tears.

"Fine." I closed the door. "If you're bored enough to clean my room, go for it." I opened the door.

I cringed. It was bad, even by my standards. He looked up at me as if he took on a job he couldn't handle.

"Hey, you volunteered." He kept looking at me. In my defense, I felt the need to say. "It came like this."

"Um." He gave the room a skeptical once over.

14

"Did you guys have fun while I was sleeping?"

"You could call it that." My voice was flat.

Her eyebrow went up in curiosity.

Zander jumped up. "We cleaned Jon's room."

Wide eyes stared back at me. "Jon cleaned his room?"

Zander's head nodded feverishly. I don't think she noticed though.

[Why do you look so surprised?] I challenged.

[I know you.] Her voice was composed

[Good point. We got bored.]

[That's pretty bored.] She insisted.

I shrugged. "I guess." Triz of confusion jumped from Zander. I rolled my eyes. [Did you know this kid asks a lot of questions?]

[Most do.] Rose smirked.

"Right. Right." I walked over to the control panel to pretend to check the monitors.

"So, did Jon remember to feed you?" She was looking at Zander.

"Yes." He grinned.

[Of course I remembered to feed him!] I was indignant.

I turned around. Her smile twitched up teasingly. I glared. Smile versus scowl, starting T minus negative two seconds and go. Can't…hold…frown…smiling is getting to me… and bang. She had won. I turned around. The controls were fine.

"You're not going that way, are you?" Zander asked.

Of course I'm going that way. No one has touched the controls since we put it on autopilot yesterday. What was he thinking?

Rose spoke before my temper flared. "Why do you ask?" Her voice was soft.

"The Tontillo space base is 14.2 light years aw..."

I stopped the ship before he could finish the sentence. I didn't realize we were this close to Drex territory. This ship must be faster than I thought. I turned around, horror-stricken.

"Who is in charge of the Tontillo space base?" I asked, careful to keep my tone even.

"My cousin Kikucolin…" Zander answered.

I waved him off. "We don't need another long, confusing name. Are they Drecian?"

He looked at the ground. "Not exactly."

"Elaborate." I commanded, while I put my hands in my pockets.

He peeked up. I guess he thought it was safe enough to continue.

"There is a division of loyalties. The Nomads believe it is wrong to imprison people from other worlds regardless of the benefiting element it adds to our museums."

[This was the precise language I had tried to avoid earlier when he mentioned his cousin's name. Seriously, how many nine-year-olds talked like this, cleaned their rooms without being asked, and helped clean someone else's room voluntarily?]

"The Idealist knows we are..."

[Did he just say we?] I asked.

Rose nodded over his head.

"...right in wanting to preserve other cultures and the surrounding worlds." Zander finished.

"Against their will?" I criticized.

"You held me against my will." He countered.

"That was different." I spat.

"Explain." He crossed his arms.

"We didn't take a mother away from her children." My voice was full of malice.

"We do not do that either." He stated promptly.

There was that *we* word again. "Sure you don't." My

sarcasm soaked my voice into a deep abyss.

Zander was hurt by my statement. Before he could say anything, I asked what the best way to get around the base would be without being caught or flying off course.

"It doesn't matter if the Martel is my cousin." The kid was dead serious.

"You do not understand." I said the words slowly.

He shook his head in confusion.

I spoke slower. "We don't want to become the museum."

Zander's eyes widened in shock. "Get out of here!"

The brat must be getting fond of us. I put the ship in reverse and scrambled into my seat. Rose quickly pulled Zander into her lap.

"Now what?" I asked.

He pulled up a map on the screen and showed us the route we needed to take. Two blue blimps popped on the radar. Rose and I locked eyes in a second of fear. Instinct kicked in, and I took Zander's path. He hadn't been lying about it being a safe route. I would have known by his Triz.

Zander's thoughts were flashes of cousins, his father, brothers, and a sister. Each thought was laced with fear.

Finally, he said, "I need to know why you're going to Drex."

[Should we tell him?] Rose asked.

"Is your cousin whatever a Nomad or Loyalist?" I asked.

Zander frowned. [Nomad.]

Rose heard his thoughts too.

[Tell him.] I told her.

She broke into a quick sketch about our mother and why we were going after her.

Zander nodded. "You may stop. Kikucolin will be of assistance."

I looked at him as if he'd just turned blue. Had he lost his mind? Being a Nomad was better, but it still might not save us since Zander was a 'we' when it came to being a Loyalist. I thought about Jaz. I couldn't see her hurting me even if our kingdoms went to war.

"Do not look at me like that." Zander attempted to order, but his voice squeaked in the middle of the sentence.

I thought about Drex weaponry and advances. The blimps were obviously closer. They would have us either way. I slowed the ship down. In no time at all, five guards were on board, staring at us fiercely. They saw we were unarmed and did not attack.

Zander stood as tall as was possible for his young body. "I am Xandermalion Avadartanrisan and wish to see your Martel."

The guards were quite surprised by this demand. It was not a request, but stated as a right.

113

"You may tell him, his cousin wishes for an audience."
Zander's authoritative tone continued.

One guard appeared to be in charge and considering the
young boy, while the others eyed each other with bits of
confusion. I was visibly nervous in my seat.

Rose was counting in her head to keep calm in a singsong
pattern. [One, two, three, one, two, three.]

"As you wish, young master." The guard in charge
bowed. Even the Drecians took notice of how dangerous their
Martel could be.

I moved the switch under the control panel unnoticed.
The switch activated a Zellian thought pattern security system I
had installed earlier while Rose was asleep. Rose and I could put
the ship on lockdown, or command it to come to a certain
destination.

"I am ready to proceed." Zander told them, as if giving
them permission to go.

One of the guards led the way back to the Drecian ship.
Rose and I shared a nervous look. This wasn't what either of us
were expecting. We followed Zander and the four other guards
followed us.

15

The guards ushered us through many long hallways. After the fifth turn, I wasn't sure if I could make my way back through this maze. Every hallway looked like the last. There wasn't anything to mark the hallway before from the one we were in.

Two guards were posted at every exit and turn. The guards wore identical uniforms, making it hard to see the differences in the guards we passed. They didn't acknowledge us. They just stood there, looking ready and distant.

Finally, we came to a hallway with a set of intricately carved doors. At least it was something different. Two men were guarding the double doors. They acknowledged the men in front of us with a nod. Each man took a door handle and opened them.

We entered into a long hallway like room. It was much wider than the ones we had been traveling through. Seven men surrounded a throne at the far end of the room.

I easily found an additional exit within seconds. It was off to my left...behind the guards. The man in the chair was obviously in charge. I glanced at Zander. It was easy to see the resemblance between the man in the throne and Zander. It was in the hair color and the way he carried himself. Maybe some Drecians are born to be a Martel.

Hanging at the side of every guard was a leather pouch. The size and shape were similar to a long knife or short sword. The guard closest to the Martel stood straighter as we entered. As he moved, the flap of his vest opened, revealing a gun. It was a newer model. So new, it hadn't made it out of this galaxy. The other guards most likely had the same kind of gun hidden away.

Zander was unscathed by all the weaponry in the room. We, on the other hand, were fully aware. I noticed Rose's breathing was shallow.

[Breathe Rose.] I instructed my sister.

[Thanks.] She sucked in a breath of air.

The Martel wasn't much older than I was, maybe five years. 22 or 23 and leading a war. Probably not the whole war, but a portion of it.

"Hello cousin Kikucolin, Martel of Tontillo." Zander told the man in charge.

"Greetings young cousin, Xandermalion Avadartanrisan future Martel." He smiled down at Zander. "What brings you such a great distance from home?"

"Father and I were on the planet MaCownia and I…

decided to explore."

The Martel chuckled.

Zander continued. "Mr. and Miss…" He gave Rose and me his attention. "I do not know your proper names."

"Julian." I supplied.

"Mr. Jon Julian and Miss Rose Julian have been kind enough to supply a ride home." Zander sounded much older than his nine years.

The Martel's intense gaze swept over my sister and moved over me until he met Zander's eyes again. "You know I can not allow them to cross my border in light of the war." He stated.

My heart sank. We were only a few days' journey away from Drex. It was too close to come and fail. This Nomad Martel didn't believe in collecting 'art'. What if he decided to kill us? My thoughts frightened Rose, making the air harder to breathe for her.

"Will you hear out their situation first?" Zander asked on our behalf.

"I will." The Martel responded. He turned to us. "Begin."

[Tell him Jon.] She couldn't find the words because the air seemed too thick for her to breathe, let alone carry on a legitimately convincing conversation.

I showed no visible distress as my heart began to race. I

usually push public speaking off to one of my sisters. A man looks another man in the eye, regardless of the consequences. I held his intense stare and prayed.

"Several years ago, about five and a half to be exact, our mother came upon the Minefield of Visions and Pains. She was separated from our father when a Drecian ship found her. The Drecian ship took our mother and her ship. We have delayed this long in coming, because of the meteor storms; otherwise we would have come three years ago."

The Martel rubbed his goatee. "You were right in bringing them here, Xandermalion Avadartanrisan."

He motioned for a guard to come forward. The guard came and leaned over to hear the Martel's whispers. [Prepare the war room.]

[That's a good thing, right?] She asked.

[I think so.] I told her.

Zander was quite pleased with himself. We waited in silence.

A few minutes later, the guard came in and told the Martel loud enough for us to hear. "The war room is ready."

The Martel slid out of the chair easily. Four guards immediately surrounded him. Two followed behind the other four guards. One guard watched with piercing eyes as we followed the Martel with the six guards. Our three guards tailed us, and the final guard trailed the end of our line. We exited out the left door into a long hallway. We made a right and walked down another long metal hallway. Each guard kept a stiff pace.

After several more turns, we finally entered a room. In the middle of the room was an oval table. I quickly counted the chairs, twelve. On the opposite side of the door, was a large screen. The Martel walked over to the screen as if he was bored. The guards lined the room around the table.

Two of them stood on either side of him ready to shield the Martel on a moment's notice. The other guards held their hands in front of them, close to their waist. It was intimidating, to say the least. Not to mention the three guards who have been trailing us the whole time. One of them took his place behind Zander, another behind Rose, and the last behind me.

"Sit. Please." The Martel gestured at the table with his left hand.

[Zander does that too.] Rose thought.

[Does what?] I asked.

[Uses his left hand.] Rose told me.

[I hadn't noticed.] I answered.

[That's odd.] Rose thought back.

[It's a hand Rose, who cares which one you use as long as the job gets done?] I replied.

Zander quickly plopped down in one of the seats closest to

119

the screen. Rose and I took seats closer to the exit out of instinct. It wasn't as if we could get very far with the seven guards in the room for the Martel, not to mention the insane amount of guards around every corner. I would hate to see how many guards were off duty right now.

"I have decided we will assist you." He picked up a remote off the table.

"You will?" I slipped.

He chuckled in return. "Of course, I have a mother myself. I would try to change her situation, as you are. With our help, you will succeed. It's a great way to reinforce our cause."

"How far are we from Drex?" Zander asked.

"Less than a day." Kikucolin gave him a wistful smile.

"I had one of my people do some research. According to the time frame you mentioned earlier, I can pinpoint your mother's probable whereabouts down to three locations."

Martel Kikucolin must have pushed a button on the remote, because the screen popped on. Three pictures of three separate buildings were on the screen. He rattled off several names I couldn't understand, before he gave us information about the most probable museum. He held out his hand, and one of the guards quickly put a rectangle object in it. He gingerly walked over to Rose and me.

"Do you know what this is?" Kikucolin asked attentively.

"A map?" I asked.

He nodded. "Present and Past." He smiled at the new toy. "Here." He sat it on the table between the two of us.

I picked it up to examine it. The basics were the same as the one Bill had. The Martel took his time walking back to the screen. He ran through the layout of the first museum.

"The layouts of this museum and of the other two museums are in the rectangular device."

"Thank you." Rose replied.

I mentally saved the one he thought was most probable. We would be going there first. This would be a challenge. Each museum was much larger than any museum I had seen.

"I would send in my people, but that would be somewhat ostentatious. We would not go unnoticed." Kikucolin frowned.

I took in the guards, Kikucolin, and Zander. We were similar enough to be mistaken as a Drecian on sight.

"We can go." I told him.

"I thought you might agree to go in without much back up." Kikucolin grinned maniacally.

[What have we gotten ourselves into?] Rose thought.

[He's on our side.] I thought back, considering his Triz carefully.

Yes, this was a small battle for the Nomads; one, that we would hopefully win. Our plight happened to align with his primary goal, which, in this case, put him on our side.

[For the moment.] Rose agreed.

[He seems genuine in his goal.] I added.

[I know.] Rose didn't like that we were in this situation where we had to trust a Drecian with our lives.

"I like museums." Zander said cheerfully.

"You do?" Kikucolin's intelligent eyes grazed over us. "You should go with them."

"I..." I froze when Kikucolin's steal glare hit me. "… think that might be better than you sneaking away later to tag along." With Zander's record, that was a real possibility.

[Good save.] Rose grinned.

[Shut up Rose.] I told her.

"One guard will be with you." Kikucolin informed us.

"Thank you." Rose's appreciative tone was met with a smile from Kikucolin.

"It's my pleasure." The Martel responded.

16

I was quite satisfied when I left the Martel. He was going to help us. We had a relatively safe way to Drex. We would find our mother.

The guards led us down several more hallways until we came to a door. We entered into a smaller room. It had several comfortable seats circling the room and two closets. On a small table were three different piles of clothing, folded neatly. Each pile had a paper in front of it. One said 'Martel's cousin', another simply read 'female', and the third 'older male'.

"Change your clothes." One of the guards ordered.

"Why?" I challenged, standing straighter.

"Because." My head turned sharply at the sound of Zander's voice. "No one in Drex would wear such an outfit unless it was Blandin Day."

"Blandin Day?" Rose asked. We had never heard of such a thing.

Zander's shoulders drooped in frustration. "Martel

Mattelion K. Blandin the first, took over Drex many millennia ago. He and his crew, and other Martel's crews dressed like people from other planets and evaded to conquer it. On Blandin Day everyone visits the museums in their costumes and makes fun of them." His voice made it sound as if that was a perfectly rational way to act.

[Does he realize we are not Drecians?] I asked Rose sarcastically.

[I think so.] Her thought was cautious and unsure. [Most of the time anyway.]

I rolled my eyes and pushed Zander out of the room, clothes in hand. The guards backed out of our way.

"Hey!" Zander exclaimed. "What are you doing?" He demanded.

"Chill, Zander." I ordered.

The guard was speechless, but his thoughts were loud. [You can't talk to a future Martel that way!]

[Wanna bet!] I thought back, although he couldn't hear. The door muffled Rose's laugh.

I looked down at Zander. "Boy, you need to learn to show women some respect."

"Huh." He was confused.

I spoke slowly, so it would sink in. "She can't change if we're in there with her."

"Oh." He blushed.

The guard caught on, finally. He opened the door across the hall. We went in and changed our clothes quickly.

[Rose?] I asked.

[Almost.] She confirmed.

I hurried out of the room and leaned against the wall, so it would look like I had been there for hours. Zander was confused again, this time by my quick movements. Just as the door closed, Rose's door opened.

[Ha ha.] She rolled her eyes. [So funny.]

My lips turned upwards.

[I can read your mind, you know?] She tapped her head in the process.

My lips went into full grin mode. [I know.]

"Come on." She rolled her eyes. I pushed away from the wall.

The guard led us away. Zander's thoughts were jumbled and unsure. I knew a question was coming.

"When I am with you two, I always get the feeling I am missing part of the conversation! Why is that?"

Rose grinned at me. I shrugged him off.

"We're twins." We said together.

He looked even more confused. Apparently, he didn't like my...our explanation.

"That's not it." Zander's voice was slow and skeptical. I shrugged again. He didn't ask any more questions about it though.

It wasn't long before I found myself in front of Martel Kilowhatsit. I started processing the room and who was in it.

[Kikucolin] Rose reminded me.

[Kik...kik..] I tried to remember how she said it.

[Kik...oo...colin] Rose thought it slower.

[Okay, Kikucolin.] I shrugged.

Behind Martel Kikucolin was a long screen. We could see outside. I didn't know what to say. To call me speechless would be an understatement. Utter shock came closer. Drex was no ordinary planet. It was magnificent and huge. MaCownia was a decent size planet, and Zelle was average, but Drex made both of them look puny.

"Ahh...Finally, I am home." Zander seemed relieved. It probably had something to do with his father.

Drex was light blue. It appeared to have a sparkle about it. I leaned forward. It had some sort of light mist surrounding the planet that shimmered. On either side of the planet, several kilometers away, was a space base similar to Kikoocol...Zander's cousin.

[Kikucolin] Rose rolled her eyes.

[Yeah, that.] I agreed.

[Jon?] Rose's thought was awed.

[I know!]

[How will we find Mom on there?] Rose's concern was a reflection of how I felt.

[Let alone rescue her.] I forced myself to swallow and breathe.

The ship descended slowly. Too slowly, it gave me more time to worry. Everyone within fifteen galaxies knows Drex is a force to be reckoned with, but only one word came to my mind... massacre. With their intellect and weapons to back up their mouths, it would not be wise to even consider doing what we were about to do.

"You can tell uncle I assisted in your return." Kikucolin smirked.

"Oh." Zander looked at the ground. "I had hoped he would not notice."

The Martel's eyebrows twirled upward. "You honestly thought he would not notice one of his son's absence?" He was appalled.

Zander nodded.

"You are mistaken, you have much to learn." Zander's cousin informed him.

Zander's head shot up rebelliously. He gave the Martel a sharp look.

The Martel laughed freely. After he was done, he turned his eyes to mine. "You have the schematics."

I held the rectangle shape up for him to see.

"Lt. Eliana, go with them." The Martel commanded.

My eyes quickly swung to the movements. A girl glided from behind one of the men. She was dressed in a similar fashion to the other guards, including the leather vest and weapon at her side.

There is something incredibly attractive about an armed woman. Her eyes were green and her hair was dark and long. Part of her hair was held back in braids, so it was out of her face. The rest hung straight to her waist.

My throat went dry. [If I had to be under guard, she is the one I wanted, shackle me now.]

[Oh brother!] Rose moaned.

I ignored her. My angel was coming my way.

"Cousin, I really do not think this is necessary." Zander whined.

"Sure it is." I jabbed him. His Triz were mortified, but I didn't care.

The Martel hid a grin. My angel let a soft smile escape her lips. She was amused by me. I can work with that.

[Jon!] Rose warned.

Reluctantly, I turned my head to face her. [What?]

She glared. [You know very well what! First a MaCownian, now a guard from Drex, what are you thinking?] Rose demanded.

[She's beautiful.] Escaped in my thoughts. [Uh....that wasn't supposed to come out.] I explained to Rose.

[I bet.] My sister's thought swam in sarcasm. Confused Triz exploded from Zander. The kid was way too perceptive.

"Ready?" The green-eyed beauty asked.

[I sure am!] "I believe so." I gave her my most charming smile. She didn't bat an eye, but her Triz continued to be amused.

17

The museum was more of a mansion. It made our ridiculously huge home seem incredibly small. In fact, if you set five mansions side by side, you would come closer to the size of this museum.

Eliana led the way. We were going to walk into the museum in broad daylight. I was beginning to get used to the apprehension weighing in the pit of my stomach. With these clothes, I did have to admit we fit in with the others passing us. During the day, we were mistaken for tourists, whereas if we had come at night, they would know we were up to something.

[Act casual.] Rose reminded.

I stood straighter and forced my apprehension down past the pit of my stomach to my toes. When I turned toward Rose, she was smiling back. Zander plodded between us.

[He thought all the dressing up and going out was some kind of game. But really, since he is a Martel's son, what trouble could he get into?] I thought to no one in particular.

[More than you can imagine.] The angel like voice blossomed in my head.

[Rose?] For the first time in days, I secured my thoughts. Her horror-stricken eyes stared at mine.

"Jon?" She gasped.

Zander stopped with us, not twenty yards away from the museum. Eliana stopped too, but she didn't turn around.

[You heard me?] Her thought electrified the air with shock. Her posture did not change.

[We heard you.] Rose replied.

Slowly, she turned around. Her lips were pursed in a straight line. Her body held the same posture as before, but her eyes were another story. The green pools were full of bewilderment. Apparently, she wasn't used to others responding to her thoughts.

"What is going on?" Zander complained.

"Nothing, nothing at all." My tone was too apathetic to be convincing.

Zander stared back at me. "What do you call nothing?" He asked knowingly.

But my attention was focused on Eliana. Zander shifted his gaze to look at her, then to me, and lastly to Rose. He didn't like what he saw.

[Whatever nothing is, it is not good.] Zander thought solemnly.

"It's fine." I brushed him off.

Zander was skeptical. My eyes didn't leave Eliana's face.

Rose squatted down. I heard the charm in her voice. "Really, everything is fine Zander." I knew the smile that went with that tone well. I saw him nod out of the corner of my eyes.

"How can you..." Eliana asked, stopping when she noticed Zander's attention was on her. [read minds?]

It didn't matter how much reassurance Rose gave him, knew something didn't add up. We were talking in half sentences that didn't make any sense. It took him all of two seconds to lose patience with us.

"Can you please tell me what is going on?" Zander whined.

"Not this time." I kept my tone even.

Rose came back down to his eye level and tried to calm him down, so we wouldn't make a scene. "Do you want to hear a secret?" He nodded. That was the perfect distraction.

[Where are your parents from?] I asked.

It was common knowledge on our planet only people from Zelle could use their thoughts to talk to others. Rose's voice muffled into the background. A perplexed Triz came from the woman in front of me. She started rattling off places on Drex and various space bases. This wasn't getting me the answer I needed.

[No. Which parent isn't from Drex?] My tone was firm.

"Huh?" Escaped from her lips. Luckily, Zander was absorbed in conversation.

[My Grandpa wasn't born on Drex.] Her tone was confused.

[Where was he from?] I demanded.

She shrugged. [He passed away years ago. My parents have been dead for a while too.]

[No siblings?] I was curious.

She shook her head no. [No cousins either.]

I closed my thoughts. She was confused when my thoughts disappeared.

[That explains it.] I told Rose.

[I heard.] Rose told me as she continued to entertain Zander.

[What did you just do?] Eliana asked.

[What was your Grandpa's name?] Rose inserted as a distraction.

[Aaron Peterson?]

My jaw dropped. "Your Grandpa was *the* Aaron Peterson!"

Rose and Zander stopped speaking. I felt a tug on my shirt. I looked down to see Zander's curious eyes.

I could answer this question. "Aaron L. Peterson is a well known Zanxtear champion from my planet."

"You know him?" Eliana was thoroughly surprised.

Zander was intrigued.

"Know him! He is...is" I stuttered.

"On a poster in your room." Rose inserted.

"You are kidding." Eliana's eyes were wide.

"Well yeah, but." I stammered.

Eliana started laughing. I sent a piercing glare to Rose.

Rose returned it with a grin. "No, I'm not." She confided. "Do you even know what a Zanxtear Race is?" Eliana shook her head no and Rose burst into laughter. [You know how to pick them Jon.]

I blushed. [Rose.] I growled.

An innocent smile popped on my sister's face. "What?" Rose asked calmly.

Eliana's eyes moved back and forth, taking us in. "Where are you from?"

"Well, where was Aaron L. Peterson from?" Rose was cryptic.

Eliana's eyes were curious and slightly suspicious. "I'm not entirely sure. Mom mentioned Landryn once, but I think it was a city." Her voice was strong, but unsure of the facts.

"We have cousins in Landryn. We just saw Jasmine a few

days ago." I offered.

"I have always been under the impression Grandpa lived far away." She gave me a pointed look.

Eliana was tired of beating around the bush; she wanted to know where we were from, now. It took three and a half days to get to Muesey and two more to get to MaCownia. From MaCownia, it took two more days to make it to Kikucolin's space base in Drex territory. From there, it took an additional day to make it to the actual planet.

"Ships go much faster than they used to." I gave her my most charming smile. She didn't buy it. To Rose I thought, [Well, at least I didn't tell her where we're from.]

[I guess.] Rose's voice sounded bored.

"May I ask you a question?" Rose directed to Eliana.

"You may." Eliana's voice was stiff.

Zander hung on every word.

[Have you ever thought talked with others?] Rose asked.

[Thought talk? That is an interesting thing to call it. No, but I can hear others' thoughts sometimes. When I'm away from the planet, I lose touch with the thoughts and feelings of others.]

[So, when you come home, here, you usually can?] Rose prodded.

Eliana nodded. [But I have been to some cities on this planet that I can not.]

[Can you usually hear thoughts in this city?]

[Yes.] Eliana replied.

[Good.] My shallow breathing became normal again.

Her brows crinkled. "Why is that good?"

[Two people from my planet have to be in close proximity to share thoughts, making the possibility that our mother is here all the more likely.] I explained.

"Are we ready?" She asked, unsatisfied with our question and not answers.

"No, I'm not!" Zander crossed his arms and pouted.

I rolled my eyes. "Of course, you are a kid." I pushed him in the middle of his back, and he walked forward with us.

He grumbled. [I want to know what is going on! Wow, is that a boomerang?] A little kid walked by us.

"We can stop by the gift shop on the way out." Rose soothed.

"Okay." He was content again.

18

We walked into the lobby. It was wide and open, with a high ceiling. A curtain, with a gold ornate floral pattern, hung from the far wall to my right, from ceiling to floor.

"Will you be needing a halo-tour today?" The receptionist caught me off guard.

"No thank you, but we will require a map." Eliana informed her.

She nodded. "Sign in."

Eliana walked down and signed her name on the screen. The receptionist looked at her own screen. She took something from under the counter and placed a rectangle object in her hands. It was six inches long, four inches wide and half an inch thick.

"Enjoy our museum, Lt." The receptionist said.

"Do you know her?" I asked as we walked out of the lobby.

"No." She turned on the object.

"Then, how did she know you are a Lt.?" I pressed.

She glanced at me. Her face turned puzzled. "You really do not know, do you?"

I shook my head no. Rose was listening intently. We began passing older exhibits.

"When I signed in, it brought up my ID information." She saw our shock. "Just the basics, though: name, parents, where you live, your work, height, weight, and eye color. Normal stuff. Hobbies are optional." Her attempt to reassure us failed miserably.

[Normal stuff?] I told Rose, leaving Eliana out.

Rose was as shocked as I was.

[Isn't your planet like that?] She had sensed our mood change.

"Um. No." I stumbled.

[We have Royalty, not Martels.] Rose thought curtly, allowing Eliana to hear.

My eyes sent daggers at my sister. I couldn't believe Rose was being so rude. She walked ahead quickly, avoiding me. I let it go.

Zander enjoyed all of the old exhibits and was ready to move on to the live ones. I was too. Dad and Jahni were counting on me. Mom had to be here somewhere. I hope.

[I hope so too.] Rose's sincerity caught me off guard. If my optimist was down to hoping, we were in trouble.

"How far until we see the people?" Zander asked eagerly.

I gave Rose a wary look. Sometimes I forgot Zander is from Drex and not Zelle.

"Ten more exhibits." Eliana answered.

"Oh." He went ahead, bouncing from glass window to glass window, not waiting long enough to push the button with the history of the artifacts.

[Do you think we're close enough to hear Mom?] Rose asked me.

[I don't know. Jahni said she used to hear her in her dreams, but it is a long way from here.]

[Let's try.] Rose implored. Eliana didn't hear us.

[Mom?] I asked the silence. I couldn't hear anything besides myself, Rose, Eliana, Zander.

"Yay. People!" Zander cheered, running to look at them. He pressed his face against the window.

"Zander, use your manners." Rose instructed.

[Eliana didn't seem bothered by us telling Zander what to do.] My thought wasn't to anyone.

"Someone needs to." She smiled at me. "He is too young to go without instruction."

[Jon! You know better.] Rose referred to my unlocked thought.

[I know Rose, but I forgot.] I sealed my thoughts, so Rose

was the only one who could hear. It wasn't hard, just tedious.

Rose rolled her eyes. [Jon, just because a beautiful girl is around doesn't mean...]

[She is beautiful, isn't she?] I glanced at her and forgot to turn around.

Her voice raised two octaves. [mean you can get distracted!] My head shot to Rose.

[Did I do something?] Eliana asked us with concern.

"No." Rose smiled. Her eyes were still dark with emotion. "Family discussion. Do you have an idea which exhibit she might be in?"

"No, I'm sorry. I'm not sure how it is organized. So far, the best I can see in the organization is dead and undead. I'm not sure if they catalog by species, age, gender, family, importance, year added to the museum, or something else."

[We got the idea.] Rose held up her hand to stop her.

I couldn't understand her today. She was being unRose and more me. Am I turning into her? The thought of turning into my sister was horrifying. I cringed.

[I'm sorry.] Rose apologized to me.

[For what?] Maybe she'd explain what was going on.

[Being a jerk to you, about the girls.] Rose explained.

[That's what's bugging you!] My thought was loud.

She was sheepish and didn't answer. Instead, she took a

few quick strides to join Zander. I decided to let it go and lag behind with Eliana.

Hi, would be lame. "So, have you been here before?" I asked.

She continued looking at the map. "Not since I was a child."

"How old are you now?" I was serious, but more than that, I wanted to hear her voice.

"Why?" She looked up suspiciously.

Aggressive. I closed my thoughts, and I gave her a crooked smile. I like that in a woman.

"Just curious." I held up my hands innocently as if to say I was weaponless. Her lip went up in an amused smile. I was still in the game.

"Old enough." She answered after a long pause. "What is your age?" She countered.

[You're hopeless.] Rose commented to me alone.

[You check out guys all the time. I just admire God's handiwork a few times and you throw a tantrum. Deal with it!] Eliana was entirely amused. It was all she could do not to bust out laughing.

[She heard that.] Rose hissed.

I caught a glimpse of her out of my left eye. She's not running away or speeding up. It might be okay.

141

"Look at this!" Zander exclaimed.

I walked over to see what was so interesting. Rose was ooing and awing at the right parts.

It was a miniature city with miniature ships. [Apparently, they didn't have very good weaponry or they would have broken the glass and escaped.] I smirked.

[Actually, each exhibit is guarded by a password protected shield.] Eliana informed us.

"Oh." I breathed out my disappointment. [So, why are we here today?]

[This is not a recon trip. We are here to find the location of your mother and gather information. We will recon another day.] She explained.

[That sounds reasonable.] Rose agreed.

"Yeah, that's pretty cool, Zander." I pushed the information button, and it started sputtering off the name, size, population, and location of the planet they came from. It ended with the question: would you like to hear about fashion, the founder, literature, machinery, people, politics, sports, weaponry, or weather?

"No, thank you." Zander replied politely and raced off to the next exhibit. We followed with far less enthusiasm.

[Mom!] Rose called. [What if she doesn't know us?]

[Dad didn't. Maybe we should call her by her first name.]

I suggested.

[Okay. Miranda! Miranda Julian!] Rose called.

[I guess we need to get closer.] I thought glumly.

She nodded soberly as she trailed Zander's fast pace.

The next glass area we crossed revealed a one-room house. All around the house was fresh grass. There was a small waterfall in the background a few yards and one tree. In front of the house, facing us, was a woman sitting in a rocking chair.

"Wow, she is pretty." Zander stopped to admire her through the glass.

[Jon!] Rose exclaimed.

[I know.] I thought back.

A woman about ten years older than us looked up. She was beautiful. Her hair lay in loose brown curls. As she walked closer, I could see her eyes. They were a deep purple.

[Do you think she heard us?] Rose asked.

[I think so.] I couldn't take my eyes off her. She looked just like the pictures I had seen on the Com. It felt like a picture coming to life.

[I heard you.] She responded. [Did you come for me?] Her voice had the same song-like quality Rose's voice had.

[You're Miranda?] I asked. She nodded.

[Do not interact too much, the security will notice.]

Eliana cautioned us.

I turned around to look at the glass case behind us while Rose pushed the button to buy us a few more minutes.

[Are you okay?] Rose pleaded.

Miranda had better conditions than our father did on Muesey. Seeing him in that cell was the worst thing I have ever been through in my life. Here we are on Drex so close, but we can't do anything about it.

[Now.] Eliana ordered.

[What?] I turned to Eliana.

[It's time to go. We will get her out soon.] Her eyes were tender and her mind flashed through images of her own mother. In her mind, she would help us just for her dead mother's sake.

[You look so young.] My mother's voice was tender and concerned.

[Old enough.] I scoffed.

[Is Alex okay?] Our mother thought desperately.

[Dad is alive and well back on Zelle.] I replied. I saw the woman's reflection gasp. [She doesn't know us Rose.]

A flood of sad Triz swept over the hallway. I wasn't sure how much belonged to me and how much was Rose. Rose knew Jahni immediately and part of me did too. Our own mother doesn't know us!

I turned around, slung my arm around Rose, and leaned

forward to push for more details about the sports of Zelle. Eliana gave me a cautious look and reminding me not to be conspicuous. She went ahead to watch Zander gawk at another clear case.

Our mother gave us a once over. [Jon, Rose? Are you really the twins?] Her voice was a mixture of confusion and awe. She didn't let us answer before asking another question. [How old are you?]

Rose was trying to hold back her tears as her lip quivered.

[We are 17.] I told her.

[17?] She exclaimed, putting a hand over her mouth. [My babies are 17! You look so grown up!]

A crooked smile jumped out. I couldn't help myself. [A minute ago, we were so young. Now, we're so old?]

[Jon, Rose, we had better go.] Eliana insisted.

[Who is that?] Our Mother asked. She had the same curious tone Jahni had. It was a tone I was used to.

[Lt. Eliana.] I responded.

[Lt. of what?] Miranda was unsure. We do not have Lt.'s on Zelle. My Mother seemed more like a Miranda than a Mom. I thought about Dad.

We turned to walk away. A continuous sad Triz came from Miranda's side of the glass. She held up a hand to wave, but dropped it. She sat back down to watch us walk from sight.

[Bye. I love you very much.] Not even the most heartless

could mistake her sincerity.

[We love you too, Mom.] Rose saved me.

I wasn't sure I loved her yet. I cared about her. I loved the idea of my mother, but Miranda was not old enough to be a Mom to two 17-year-olds, let alone a 20-year-old! In a few months, she will be a Grandma!

Eliana chanced a brief look my way. [Your mother's very pretty.]

[Thank you.] My thought was dull.

Eliana looked at me curiously, but stayed quiet.

I wasn't so lucky with Rose. [Jon, why did you call her Miranda?]

[She didn't hear me, did she?] I didn't want to hurt her feelings.

[No.] Rose waited for my answer.

Zander pushed several buttons at once and hurried along to push more buttons, so the hallway clamored with useless noise.

"This is fun!" Zander cheered.

"Slow down." I ordered. He stopped running. He placed his hands to his side as he moved his feet quickly.

[Jon?] Rose refused to let it drop.

I stifled a groan. [Fine. You saw her.]

[Yeah. So?] She asked.

[She's not much older than we are and Jahni is even closer

to her age.]

[Dad is just as young.] Rose reminded.

[I guess.] I thought, not really agreeing.

[What is the difference?] She protested.

I waited long enough for Rose to start losing her patience.
[The difference is...]

Crap! What is the difference? I thought about the past
three and half years. I've grown up a lot. Dad had the talk with
me. He was there to teach me about Shuttle Cars, watch races
with me, and he has been at every single race I have competed in
cheering me on. He has just been there. Jahni has been the Mom
and older sister all in one.

[I'm not ready to say I love her yet. I will not say it until I
mean it.]

"Oh." My sister replied, not fully understanding. Rose
loved almost everyone immediately.

A few minutes later, Rose took charge of Zander and
followed him as he ooed and awed over every little detail.

[Does that ever get weird?] Eliana matched my steps.
[Sharing your thoughts with everyone?]

[Not really. It's not with everyone, just Rose.] I
explained.

[Oh.] Eliana sounded confused.

[Rose is my twin.] I added.

[Really?] Eliana's thought held a hint of shock.

I was curious. [Who did you think was older?]

She smiled an, 'I'm not replying smile.'

I rolled my eyes. [We've been everywhere together. I'm used to Rose in my head. The few things I want to keep to myself are pointless. She can read my body language just as easily as she can my thoughts; go figure.]

I thought about the girl stuff and tried not to hurl. I still wasn't used to what went on in her head when it came to guys and...the other stuff. I made a face.

[We give each other privacy, kind of.] I continued.

[What does *kind of* mean?] Eliana asked.

[I can shut Rose out, and she can shut me out, but it is easier not to. If she accidentally thinks something, I can cover it so no one else realizes she thought it. She isn't rude. You know those people who tease you when you say something stupid?]

[Yeah.] Eliana responded.

[Rose doesn't. It's okay to think my way and for her to think her way.]

[That's nice.] Eliana contemplated the idea of being accepted for who she was.

I did a double take. Had someone tried to force their own thoughts on her? I wasn't sure, so I asked.

[But no one heard your thoughts growing up. How can

they change them, if they don't know what you're thinking?]

[People...will try to make you think a certain way even if they do not have the privilege of knowing your thoughts. You both are lucky.] She was whimsical.

[Uh...thank you.] I stuttered.

Eliana's statement stunned me. Eliana seemed so put together. She was beautiful, intelligent, and careful. Careful...sometimes people are careful, because they have been hurt.

Zander's giggles echoed in the hallway.

[I love you Jon!] Rose thought happily.

I rolled my eyes and grinned. [You too Rose.]

My sister giggled.

[See what I mean, no peace and quiet!] I teased. Eliana laughed an elegant laugh, a poem all its own.

"I'm tired!" Zander proclaimed.

"Uh, buddy, you should have said something a while ago. We have quite a bit to go before we're back. You're going to have to tough it out." I told him.

Zander was too tired to care and ignored me, but he didn't whine. Eliana checked the map and found a quicker route. The ooing and awing had disappeared. Rose tried, but couldn't talk him out of his depressed mood either.

[I think he needs a nap.] Rose confided.

His feet drug on the ground. Ten minutes later, his eyes started blinking. Zander stumbled a few times. At this rate, he would be curled up in a ball, sleeping in the middle of the museum. I wonder if they'd put him in the lost and found. I thought smugly.

"How far?" I asked.

Eliana looked down at the map. "A little over a kilometer."

He'd never make it. "Come here Zander."

Zander stopped. I scooped him up. He had his arms around my neck, his legs around my waist, and his head on my shoulder. It didn't take him long to fall asleep.

The first two minutes of carrying him was a piece of cake. After that, it got more difficult as we went. I was not about to sit down in front of Eliana and look like a whip. I had no other choice; I steeled my arms and kept walking. My arms would be sore tomorrow. It was a good thing Zander had an iron grip on my neck.

"Do you want me to carry him for a bit?" Eliana offered.

"I got it." I told her immediately, wondering if I could make it all the way to the front of the building.

Rose didn't bother to offer. She only smiled like she had a secret as we headed back. I focused on each step I was making, telling myself it was the last one. It kept me going until we finally reached the lobby.

Eliana turned in the map and signed the screen confirming its return. The receptionist smiled attentively towards Zander. We passed the gift shop on the way out.

"We better get him something." Rose froze in front of the gift shop.

"Zander?" I asked.

He didn't answer.

"I think we better pick it out." Eliana said.

"I'll wait here." I sat down on the ledge outside of the gift shop. Zander still clung to me. He looked peaceful while he slept. It wasn't long before the girls came out with a bag.

"Get something good?" I asked them when they approached.

"Yeah, we did." Rose grinned. "It's a talking holographic city. It even shows a mock battle."

"Cool." I stood up and opened the door with my back and let Eliana and Rose head out first.

We walked to the Shuttle Car. It was similar to a Vaktow, but it had two bunk beds protruding from the wall. Eliana said it was called a Keat after the man who designed it. I have never heard a stranger name in my life. If I designed a Shuttle Car, I wonder if they would call it the Julian Space Mobile, or J and R.

I laid Zander on the bottom bunk. He curled up and

continued sleeping. My arms ached. This was the farthest I've carried anything more than 5lb's in my life.

"Where to?" I placed my hands on the back of Eliana's chair and leaned over her.

[We need to report to Kikucolin.] She replied.

"Why do you do that?" Rose asked. She sensed Eliana's puzzlement, so she added. "Call him Kikucolin and not Martel."

"Oh, that." Eliana said it like a confession.

Yeah, that. Now that Rose mentioned it, I was curious. In her thoughts, he was always Kikucolin, not Martel, as it was in everyone else's mind. Even in Zander's thoughts, Kikucolin was cousin or Martel cousin Kikucolin.

"I know him fairly well." Eliana stated, as if it was a simple fact.

Well! How well is well? Is she trying to drive me crazy? This overpowering surge came from nowhere. I have never felt anything like it in my life. I wanted to hurt Kikucolin. I gripped the seat a little tighter. My thoughts were sealed.

Maybe not hurt him, per se. A force of unwelcome ration sunk in. I decided it would be better to drop him off on a frozen planet with no supplies. Okay, that might be harsh too, but I can't very well beat his face in with fifty guards around at all times. I forced down my anger to a tolerable level.

Why is the jerk…she is gorgeous why wouldn't he want

to… And I guess he looks okay for a dude, but I am much better looking. Why not me! She could pick me, but he is a Martel, which means prestige and a career upgrade.

"How well?" I purred.

Rose gave me a sharp stare. [I've never seen you like this.] She kept Eliana out of the loop.

[That may be, because I have never felt like this!] I growled.

[Jon! Snap out of it!] My sister's tone was so direct, I almost did.

[I can't.] I barked.

The feeling was simmering in the pit of my stomach. It was about to come to a boil. It was a good thing *he* wasn't around. I would have thrown him on the ground by now.

"I have known him for years. My father took care of his father's Shuttle Cars. We used to play when he became bored."

"Wasn't he kind of old for you?" My voice stressed.

Eliana caught a glimpse of me when she looked up. A gigantic smile crossed her face. I forgot to breathe. She is gorgeous when she smiles. I don't think gorgeous is a strong enough word, but it will have to do for now. What was I thinking about? Oh yeah, Eliana and Kik…*him*. My stomach started boiling again, and I scowled.

"Jon." Eliana spoke my name calmly.

A chill ran through my body. My name sounded so good on her angelic lips. What was I...oh yeah. She is too distracting. The feeling returned a third time. It felt like I was on one of those rides where you soar into the air long enough to feel peace and then plummet to your almost death.

"I do believe." She hedged. "You are jealous."

Jealous? Was I jealous? My eyebrows furrowed together.

"Why would I be jealous?" I attempted nonchalance and failed miserably. Maybe I am jealous.

"You tell me." Eliana smiled innocently and drove us closer to *him*.

This conversation was not taking a good turn.

"I thought as much." Eliana replied smoothly and focused on going forward.

I was so angry; I was about to blow. How could I ever have thought she was interested in me? Maybe I'm not as good looking as I thought. Nah, that isn't it. So what does *he* have that I don't?

"Kikucolin and I are *just* old friends." She attempted to pacify me.

Friends, huh? The anger slipped back a little. Does that mean I still have a chance?

"I like to keep my options open." Eliana crushed my dream before it had time to grow.

That doesn't sound much better. "So what kind of guy are you looking for?"

[Pushing it!] Rose warned. [Can't you see she is toying with you?]

[She is?] I asked.

Rose nodded. And I fell for it!

Eliana answered anyway. "I suppose I am looking for a man that is not a wimp."

"Huh?" I asked. I wasn't sure if that was an actual answer. How do you define what a wimp is?

"The last three men who were interested in me could not make it past round one of the Mascousch Tournament."

"What's that?" It sounded fun, and if Eliana would be the one watching, it would be all the better.

"A team of two people go up against each other. They each have an object that represents their city, base, or planet. They hide it where their opponent can see it. Each team stands across from the other when they start the Tournament. They can do anything short of killing their opponents to get over to the other side and find the object. Many different kinds of Martial Arts are used in the competition. If the opponent is knocked unconscious, it is easier to find the object and win."

"I bet." Rose eyed me.

[What?] I asked.

[You are not going to put your life on the line just to impress a girl.] My sister was appalled.

[I would nev...] Okay, maybe I would, and Rose knew it too. [We won't be here that long.]

My sister continued glaring. Apparently, that wasn't the right answer.

[You promised Jahni.] Rose reminded me.

[What did I promise?] I asked, although, I already knew what she was getting at.

[You told her you would keep me safe. That means you need to be safe too!] Rose pushed her thought at me.

[Fine.] I agreed reluctantly.

We were at the base. Eliana turned off the Shuttle Car and stood up. Rose hadn't stopped glaring at me. I averted my gaze. Zander climbed down from the bed and rubbed his eyes.

"They also need to be taller than me." Eliana winked and left me gawking.

I am taller than she is! I still have a chance. [Rose, you coming?]

[Sure, you do.] Rose growled. "But is the real Jon coming?" She hissed.

I ignored her and followed Eliana. Zander ran to catch up. I sensed Rose coming from the angry Triz encompassing her.

19

"We found her." Eliana's voice was dull and almost seemed bored.

"Good. What do you think is the best way to recon?" Kikucolin asked.

"I believe we will need an inside man. We need passwords, keys, and a way to delete the memory on the monitors." Eliana spouted off the list.

Kikucolin nodded as he absorbed the information. It dawned on me, that this was the usual. If this was the usual, then maybe, just maybe, we could get back home safely. One of the guards was jotting down notes and ran off with the wave of Kikucolin's hand. They already knew what to do.

It was incredibly frustrating knowing where our mother was and having to wait instead of going in, busting down a few doors, and breaking glass. I was ready to be home with this whole ordeal over. Mom would be with us. Dad wouldn't be sad anymore. Jahni wouldn't feel guilty. I wouldn't have to worry about anything. I let out a breath, wishing the week away wouldn't do any good. I continued pacing our room.

[Jon, you're making me dizzy.] My sister complained.

I stopped and looked at Rose; she was sitting on her bed watching me. I had been so focused, I barely knew she was there.

"Sorry." I apologized.

We could have had separate bedrooms, but we opted to stay together. Zander demanded the room across from us. He had become the annoying little brother I never had or wanted.

"It's only a couple days." Rose assured me.

[In a couple of days, we could be halfway into the next galaxy.] I reminded her.

[I know.] There was a knock on the door.

[It's Zander.] I told Rose. The door squeaked open and his head came in.

"Are you two attending dinner?" Zander asked happily.

"There is nothing better to do." I grumbled.

"That sounds fun." Rose pasted a smile on and took his hand.

Rose wanted to be home too. I think my emotional uneasiness was affecting her more than the waiting. Two more days. We can handle two more days; I tried to convince myself. About that time, I smelled the aroma of delicious food and lost my train of thought.

20

"I want to come too!" Zander moaned.

"You can't come." I stuffed my possessions into my bag. He followed me around the room as I gathered more loose clothing.

"Why not?" Zander whined. "I will be really good. I promise."

"You can't go into the museum with us. You won't be able to keep up." I stated. The facts won't lie. His legs were too short. "I had to carry you back last time."

"It is so boring here!" Zander moaned.

"Boring?" I looked at him out of the corner of my eye. How could this place ever be boring? Stiff and formal, sure.

[It is not boring.] "I would rather be with you!" Zander pleaded.

I stopped. No one had ever said anything like that to me. I pulled a shirt off the banister.

"Please, Jon!" Zander begged.

"What did Rose say?" I was cautious, as I zipped up the bag.

"She said, whatever you say goes." His voice started getting excited.

[Rose?] I reached my Triz out to my sister.

I heard laughter. [I guess Zander found you.]

[Yeah, you can say that.] I sulked.

Zander looked up at me expectantly.

[So what did you tell him?] Rose asked.

[Still deciding.]

[So you wanted my opinion?] Rose guessed.

[Do you really have to ask?]

She laughed. [I guess not. It is okay with me, as long as he stays in the Shuttle Car.]

"Do you think you can stay in the Shuttle Car?" My tone was uncompromising.

"Thank you!" Zander fought to keep his hands to himself instead of throwing them around me. I shook my head and walked out the door. He followed me and stopped when I did.

"Well, go grab your stuff." I ordered.

Zander ran into his room and was out within ten seconds. It figures, the neat freak would be already ready to go. He hurried beside me to match my steps.

Rose was waiting for us with Eliana. They both seemed

quite happy. There was a change in mood when Rose thought about Eliana. I couldn't help looking skeptical. My sister laughed.

[You should see your face.] Rose smiled at me.

Rose played it back for me. I cringed. She was right; my emotions were too easy to read. I pushed past them and threw my stuff on the top bunk bed. Zander tailed me happily. I took his bag and put it on top with mine.

Rose and Eliana came in next, giggling. Rose kept me in the dark. I gave her a puzzled look, and they started laughing more. Girls! Ugg! I sat down. Zander climbed into the seat closest to me, grinning bigger than I had ever seen.

21

We stopped in the museum parking lot close to the door. It was dark, only one of the moons spared a little light over the gigantic building. Small squares of light followed the path up to the door and around the building.

"Zander." Eliana spoke his name.

"Yes." Zander replied eagerly.

"You must stay in the Shuttle Car." Eliana's tone left no room for doubt.

"I will." Zander grinned.

"You should be able to see what is going on here." Eliana pointed to the large screen. "It will be finalized in a moment."

"How does it work?" I was curious.

"I installed a remote inside the control panel yesterday. Our inside guy should have already installed one on his side. Once they are activated, the monitors should be transferred from their monitors to ours." Eliana explained.

"Sweet!" I grinned at her.

She smiled at me.

"I have one question." Rose's voice was concerned.

"What is that?" Eliana's tone was guarded.

"What about the security?" Rose asked.

Eliana held up a thin rectangular object. "I have all the codes we will need in here." She put it back in her pocket. "About an hour ago, our guy took each security guard a hot drink with a sleeping mixture in it. They should be asleep for the next three hours."

Rose let out a loud sigh. "Good."

Eliana led the way to the door, Rose followed closely behind her, and I took the end of the line, mimicking her movements to hide in the shadows. When she reached the door, she looked at the rectangle and typed several keys onto the keypad.

The night was pleasant and mysterious in a way I had not experienced even on Muesey. The night air was warm against my skin. The breeze made the heat bearable. The sweet smell of the plants surrounding the museum filled the air.

I leaned back on the glass and peered through the window. A guard was sprawled on the floor and another at the desk with his face down in several piles of papers. The sleeping mixture actually worked.

The keypad let off a muffled beep. Eliana looked up and

gave us a dazzling smile. I wanted to think it was meant for me. I stepped on the 'open door' sign and waited for Eliana and Rose to enter before me.

[Thank you, sir.] Eliana curtsied in her leather pants. Her hair swayed a mixture of braids and loose hair around her hips.

[Thank you…sir.] Rose mocked and rolled her eyes.

[You both are most welcome.] I grinned.

We quickly scanned the lobby for anything significant. Rose stumbled upon some security monitors. They were all blank.

[This is good.] Eliana was looking over Rose's shoulder. [It means we did it right.]

"What's that?" Rose asked at one of the screens.

A blinking red box was demanding some attention. Eliana touched her finger to the screen, and the box came off the screen and into the air. It was much bigger, and it was in countdown mode. We had thirty-five minutes before something happened. Eliana messed with the rectangle for a few seconds. Her Triz was covered in despair. It was not looking good at all.

"I cannot find the code!" She put her finger on the red box and drug it off the screen. A key pad appeared, and she began typing frantically.

[Thirty-one minutes and twenty-nine seconds.] Rose thought.

Eliana continued typing furiously. I was doing the mental calculation in my head and we were cutting it close. There was no guarantee she would find the right password. I grabbed her shoulder and pulled her away from the screen.

[We have to go now.] I thought firmly. [You are the only one with the codes.]

She gave a backward glance. The countdown said thirty minutes, fifty-eight seconds. She nodded. We rushed out of the lobby into the actual museum.

It was a good thing Rose had helped me train for the Zanxtear Race; I thought as we rushed down another hallway. Eliana was in good shape too. We ran together like three well-oiled spokes. Every few hallways, we had to pause a few seconds so Eliana could type in another password. This place was a fortress!

As we came closer, we started thinking to Miranda and calling for her. We didn't get any response. Maybe she was asleep, but at least we would hear her dreams, right? Although, I do need to be closer to Dad to hear him. That has to be it! Ugg, could this be any harder?

As we approached her glass case, we saw her waiting for us. She smiled big, and we could finally hear her thoughts.

[You came back!] Miranda thought eagerly.

[Of course we came back.] Rose replied.

166

[We didn't travel to this galaxy for nothing.] I thought.

[Are you ready?] Eliana started entering the 29-digit password. [You will have exactly thirty-seconds to walk out of the glass case.]

Miranda slung a bag over her shoulder and waited by the exit. As soon as the door slid open, she moved gracefully through the opening. We raced toward the closest exit. It was almost two miles away with all the turns. We needed to find another way out. We wouldn't reach the lobby in time.

[This way looks faster.] Eliana pointed down a different hallway than the one we had come through.

[Okay.] I agreed.

The four of us ran in the direction Eliana had pointed. When we rounded the next corner, we saw a man slumped in the seat of a cart. We lifted him out of the cart and sat him against the wall. It took us all of three seconds to climb in and drive off.

The man slept through the whole ordeal. I have expected him to wake up and scream at us to bring back his cart. Eliana turned around each corner with speed and sharp, smooth, decisive turns. I checked my watch; our thirty-minute window had seven minutes left. It didn't help that we had to stop every few yards to type in an excessively long password, especially when each hallway had a different password.

The night guards were still incapacitated when we made it

back to the lobby. We made it! We drove towards the exit and the automatic door opened. We drove the cart outside into the parking lot. We rushed to the entrance of the Shuttle Car. The door flew open and two armed guards stood holding weapons at us. I froze instantaneously, and so did the others.

[But how?] Rose moaned.

I didn't have time to think as nine other guards came from our rear. I fought to breathe evenly. I stood straighter and waited. I heard a muffled cry from the inside. They must have found our stowaway.

I focused on Zander's thought pattern. He was trying to tell them who his father was. The same stuff he said when we found him. But hey, we are on Drex now. Maybe he might actually be of help. Although, there is the whole *we* being Loyalist thing.

"You might want to listen to the kid." I forced my voice to sound bored.

The men in front of us sent piercing glares our way. One of the men motioned for them to bring Zander out of the Shuttle Car. Rose let out a sighed relief and I held mine in. This was our only chance. If Zander's father was someone they would listen to, we might not be in as much trouble.

As soon as the man holding Zander took his hand away from Zander's mouth, he started talking nonsense. It must have made sense to the men holding the weapons, because their eyes were round with shock. They let go of Zander quickly and started muttering apologetically.

"That's what I thought." Zander proclaimed.

[I think we are rubbing off on him. I believe that was the first time his grammar wasn't perfect.]

[I think it's the second, but you are definitely rubbing off on him.] Rose nodded in agreement. Eliana coughed in her hand to mask a laugh.

"Take him to his father immediately. I will deal with these thieves." His tone was just as malicious as his thoughts.

We would be dead in less than twenty-four hours once Zander left. The guard was already devising several ways to torture us. I couldn't breathe. Rose gulped. Eliana fought to keep her emotions in and succeeded. The years she had worked to become Lt. had paid off in that.

"You will not deal with them." Zander spat at them. The others looked to their leader for confirmation of what to do. "My father will want to see them." Zander stood straight, looking very dignified. He had said the magic words.

"Fine. Take them to Martel Kaltavon." He proclaimed in a threat.

They ushered us into our Shuttle Car pushing us to the back, where they forced us to sit on the floor. They stood hovering above us. Eliana sat beside me.

"Thank you Zander." I told him.

Rose nodded fervently in agreement and started to talk, but was interrupted.

"Be quiet!" One of the men hissed.

[No problem. Yes, sir.] I saluted him behind his back. Rose held her hand to her mouth to hold the giggle in. An amused smile escaped Eliana's lips.

22

"Hello Father." Zander's boyish eyes hit the ground.

This is Zander's father! He wasn't kidding about his father causing trouble for us when we first met. This man was big and intimidating, with shoulders two feet wide. He stood a few inches taller than my six two. I am not used to looking up to anyone, eye level sure, down definitely. His suit strained from the thickness of his arms when he moved.

"Hello son. You were supposed to be in your room." He condemned.

"Sorry sir." Zander apologized.

"What was your reasoning?" The Martel's tone was even.

"To have an adventure, sir." Zander peeked up.

"Was your mission a success?" The Martel inquired.

"It was sir." Zander replied.

He lifted up Zander's chin. "Next time, you will inform me of your desire for an adventure."

"Really?" Zander exclaimed excitedly.

The Martel fought back a smile. After the initial scare, he was quite proud Zander found his way home.

The Martel spoke sternly. "You are young. A guard or two needs to be with you at all times."

"Yes, sir." Zander responded eagerly.

The Martel patted him on the head. His attention refocused on us. "Now, what should I do with you?"

"They took care of me." Zander beamed.

I was thankful Zander hadn't mentioned being tied up when we first 'took care' of him.

The Martel's gaze shifted to his son for a moment. "It seems I have reason to be grateful."

We remained silent. I was unsure where this would end. I was not familiar with Drecian customs of gratitude.

"I will grant you each a request." He appraised us. "What do you choose?"

My eyes fired shock. I kept my mouth firmly closed.

"We would like our mother to come home with us for good." Rose's voice was gentle.

Martel Kaltavon motioned a guard forward and whispered orders. After the guard walked away, he turned to us. "Granted." He turned to me. "And you?"

[Thank you Rose.] I heard my mother's thought attempting to hold back the tears.

172

[You're welcome Mom. I love you.] Rose's tone was like sunshine.

[It actually worked.] Eliana's surprise entered the atmosphere.

Rose and I wanted the same thing. [What do I choose?]

[Whatever you want.] Rose enthused.

I want a safe way home. If another Martel finds us, he or she can just as easily throw us behind glass or kill us. This would all be pointless.

"I want a treaty." My voice was firm and held the air of royalty.

The Martel's eyebrow shot up curiously. "What might this treaty say?"

"That Drex will no longer add the people of my world to your museums, or entrap them in any way, and all those from my planet will be released to return with us."

"Interesting." He was thoughtful. "I can only agree for the Loyalist party. We would need a Nomad to sign for the rest of Drex."

"You are willing?" I was dumbfounded.

"I am willing." Martel Kaltavon replied smugly.

"Would you grant safe passage for the Nomadic Martel and his guards?" I asked.

He contemplated my words. "We will." He used the

173

plural for his party.

"Then you have my gratitude in return." I responded.

"Which Nomadic Martel do you choose?" Kaltavon's eyes were thoughtful.

"Martel Kik." I looked at Zander.

"Kikucolin." He supplied.

"I believe, Martel Kikucolin will agree to come." My voice was sure.

Zander's father gave me a huge smile. "So you have met my nephew, the rebel?"

We nodded.

He waved a guard to him. "Send a message to Martel Kikucolin requesting his presence for the signing of this treaty. Include a note of safe passage." The guard left immediately.

23

Kikucolin strode into the room with seven guards. His long, black leather coat hovered an inch above the floor. Zander's father's guards held the glare of Kikucolin's guards.

"Greetings Uncle, Kaltavon Martel of Martels." He bowed slightly.

"Sit." Zander's father ordered, and Kikucolin did. "I assume you can speak for the Nomadic group?"

"You assume correctly. I have contacted the other Martels, and they have consented to this treaty." Martel Kikucolin was distant.

Zander's father nodded his approval. He motioned a guard forward. "Has all of the beings from Zelle been gathered?'

"Yes, sir." He bowed. "They are waiting for a ship to take them." [All 129 of them!] He thought to himself.

[Rose?] I asked.

[That is more than I was expecting.] She thought back. [Where are we going to put them?]

Kikucolin read the treaty and motioned one of his guards forward. The guard read the treaty and nodded in approval. Zander's father signed the treaty, and Kikucolin signed the treaty.

"It is your turn." Zander's father slid the treaty to me.

I read the treaty thoroughly while Rose listened to it intently. It mentioned everything I requested.

[Read the last part again.] Rose requested.

A person from Zelle will be required to meet on Drex once a year for the annual seven-day meeting. This person will make contact with Drex a minimum of twice a year. Failure to do this without a written appeal will make this treaty void. Prince Jon Julian will be the first ambassador of Zelle to Drex. He may appoint someone of his choosing to be his replacement when the time comes he is unable to do so.

[They want me to be an ambassador?] I was baffled.

[Why not? Jahni has Jareneiks covered.] Rose encouraged.

[You think I can do it?] I was less than sure.

[I know you can.] She was optimistic.

I signed my name.

Zander's father handed the treaty to a guard. "We will need two more copies immediately. The guard bowed out of the room.

He returned quickly with two additional copies.

Kikucolin handed the treaty off to the same guard who had read it before. When he was done rereading the document, he confirmed it was the same as before. This treaty was just as important to them as it was to me. It was the first official break in what they were fighting for.

24

We walked into a crowded room. Everyone was talking loudly. The guards waited by the exit. Several in the crowd turned to look at us as we entered. Thoughts yelled question after question. I wasn't sure what was louder, their voices, or their thoughts.

[A few more minutes of this, and I am going to have a migraine.] I complained.

If I am going to be an ambassador, I suppose I had better start with my own people. I walked onto a small platform. Some of them stopped talking altogether, but their thoughts were very active. Eliana stood by the door as if she was guarding it. Rose was closer to the platform, with mother by her side.

"I am Prince Jon Julian of Zalnorel on the planet Zelle." The rest of them stopped talking, and the majority of their thoughts focused on me. "I have just signed a treaty with Drex. They have consented to let all of you return home."

"What if we do not wish to return?" A middle-aged man

in the back responded quietly.

Thoughts exploded from everyone. It had never occurred to me that some of them might want to stay. Rose gave me an encouraging smile.

"How many of you wish to stay on Drex?" I asked. Eight people raised their hands. "May I ask why?"

The middle-aged man started talking. "I was born here. My wife and children are here."

I nodded. That was reasonable. "Where are your wife and children?"

"My wife is at our home in Bandelia. My daughter is with me, and my son is with his mother." The man spoke with humility.

"Does your daughter wish to remain on Bandelia?" I inquired.

The man looked down at a little girl, maybe Zander's age. She nodded at her father. Two down, six to go. The other stories were similar to the man's. They had all been born here.

"I will see what I can do. Do the eight of you consider yourself Drecian or Zellian?" I asked.

Drecian four thoughts burst out. Both the other four claimed. Great! It was split down the middle.

[Eliana?] I loved her name. It put a smile on my lips.

[One of these days, you're going to make me puke.] Rose

complained.

[Hey, that's my line.] I smirked. It was easy to keep everyone out of the conversation when it was just Rose and I.

[Yes?] Eliana answered.

[Do you think Martel Kaltavon will let them stay?] I asked her.

[I really do not know.] Her tone was hopeful.

[Can I see him concerning the treaty?] I needed to know.

[Under code 1-732-8 of Drecian Law, it states any treaty can be brought up for discussion among the signees only.] Eliana educated me.

[Is Kikucolin still here?] I thought.

[He is leaving tomorrow.] She responded.

[I need to see him.] I stated with certainty.

Eliana turned away and whispered to the guards. They seemed to accept what she was saying. One of the guards left. She turned around and smiled.

"Do you have any other questions?" I was unsure of what to do next.

"When do we leave?" A woman towards the front asked.

"As soon as we can find a ship to accommodate all of you." I told them.

[We leave tomorrow.] Eliana smiled brilliantly in my direction. Rose gave her a disgruntled sideways glance.

[What time?] I asked.

[Fifteen hours from now.] She answered.

"We should be able to leave within fifteen hours." I stepped off the stage.

Several eyes followed my body. The talking erupted when I stepped away from the middle of the stage. They all had so many thoughts and concerns about going home. Most of them were happy and excited. Some were worried and concerned.

The guard returned. "They can see you now."

I feigned a smile at my family and followed the guard.

[I am so proud of you, Jon. I never imagined you would do something this great.] My mother oozed.

[You rock!] Rose cheered.

[Thanks.] I muttered back.

It didn't take long before the guard stopped outside a door. He opened the door without a sound. Each man sat in a big bulky chair beside one another, drinking out of an ornately carved glass. They stopped talking as I entered.

I stopped just inside the door and waited. The guard closed the door silently behind me. Martel Kaltavon finally motioned me forward. I took a seat across from them.

After a long moment, Zander's father spoke. "Is there something we can do for you?" One eyebrow cocked upward.

He was just as intimidating as before. For some odd

reason, it sharpened my senses. I leaned forward, eager to begin.

"I have talked to my people. The majority of them are ready to leave immediately. Although, there is a small group of eight beings that were born on Drex that wish to stay here."

Kikucolin scratched his beard in amusement. He didn't appear worried in the slightest.

"What do you have to say about this, nephew?" The Martel of Martels asked.

Kikucolin had a gleam in his eye. "I say it is reasonable and acceptable."

Martel Kaltavon looked me over. His thoughts were stern and closed off. I didn't know how he did it. I didn't know it was possible for someone not from Zelle to do that. In most minds, people allow themselves to go free. His thoughts were tight and closed. Maybe it was something that came with his particular rank, learning to keep your thoughts to yourself.

"They may stay." Martel Kaltavon spoke finally.

"Thank you." I smiled. "May I ask one more question?"

"Another." He was surprised.

"Yes, when do you need me back on Drex?" I grinned.

He smiled. "In 98 more days, we will be holding our annual meeting. As long as you are here on that day, you will be fine."

"Thank you." I said politely.

"Is there anything else, Prince Julian?" He smirked.

"No, thank you."

"Then if you will excuse us we were in the middle of something." Martel Kaltavon dismissed me.

"Yes, thank you for your time, Martel Kaltavon and Martel Kikucolin." I managed to keep in my desire to yell and jump for joy.

I left the room quickly and was followed by the same guard that had escorted me to the Martels. I was back in the room within minutes. My people were still chattering among themselves.

"How did it go?" My mother asked.

I smiled. "Good." I noticed it had gotten relatively quiet again. Several eyes were focused in my direction. I held up a finger. "Give me a second." I walked back onto the platform.

"I have talked to Martel Kaltavon and Martel Kikucolin." I paused to take in their reaction. They were anxious. "They have agreed to let the eight of you stay if you wish." I heard several sighs of relief. "We are leaving tomorrow."

Cheers erupted. I glanced over at my family and caught a glimpse of Eliana. She was smiling at me. I sent a crooked smile her way.

My sister cleared her throat in my head. I turned back to the crowd and told them what time to be ready. After the cheers died down, the talking started louder than before.

25

"Are you sure you must go?" Zander pleaded.

I hid a smile, "Yes, my father and sister are waiting for us."

"Oh." Zander looked down at the ground, pouting. "Can I go with you?"

"I believe Martel Kaltavon would like you to stay home for a while." I avoided his question.

"After all, you did get your adventure." Rose charmed him.

He looked up, smiling. "I did, didn't I?"

With Zander, it was hard not to notice his grammatical contraction. He walked us to the ships. We would be taking ours back, and Eliana was taking the others. When we passed MaCownia, I would mentally order our first ship to follow us to Zelle. I didn't want to stop and try to sell our junker. I was too anxious to get home.

"Are you sure I have to stay?" Zander pleaded.

I nodded.

Rose came down to his eye level. "Jon will be back soon."

"Okay!" Zander's whole mood shifted, and he seemed content after that.

It was a flurry of excitement as everyone loaded onto the ships. Miranda was on our ship along with two other families. Zander tried to stowaway only once, but I found him, and told one of the closest guards to watch him.

We would need to fuel up twice, once on the edge of Drecian space and the second when we were within a few hours of Zelle.

26

[We are almost out of fuel.] Eliana thought from the other ship.

I checked the gauges. We had a little while before we needed to fuel, but if we fueled up now, we would be able to make it all the way to Zelle.

[Where do you want to stop?] I didn't know the area well.

[Yazil is the closest. They are a basic trade planet. It should be easy to land and leave.] Eliana offered.

[Sweet.] I thought back.

I followed Eliana's lead to Yazil.

It didn't take long for my ship to fuel up. I walked over to Eliana. She was busy hiring one of the locals to fuel the second ship.

We were so close to home. I couldn't wait to see Jahni again. Dad would be ecstatic to finally have Mom safely home.

Eliana turned to me. "It will take us a few hours to finish fueling up. You can go home with your mother. We will meet you on Zelle." She smiled.

[Are you sure?] I was anxious to leave.

[Absolutely.] Eliana assured me.

[You're the best!] I gave her a quick hug. She smiled again.

Rose walked over and leaned against the fueling station. She rolled her eyes. I had the feeling I was being chaperoned. We were pulling away from the planet within minutes.

27

"You're my Jahni?" Mom was shocked.

"How did you get so... so?" She gestured to Jahni's
stomach, which was sticking out just enough to announce to the
world a baby was on its way. They were both crying hysterically.
My sister grabbed Joe's hand and pulled him over.

Mom gave him a once over. "Joseph?" She was
incredulous.

Jahni laughed, and he smiled. He nodded a yes.

"Oh my! I missed you so much!" The tears fell in pools
and a lot more hugging went on. "Tell me everything!" She
demanded happily. Jahni giggled hysterically through her own
tears. This wasn't how we pictured it, but in a way, it was.

About that time, Dad opened the door and came out
casually. He had his hands filled with a small pile of papers he
was reading. He was so engrossed in what he was reading that he
didn't hear us at the bottom of the stairs. Mom looked up and
saw him. Somehow, she managed to smile deeper.

"Alex?" He looked up, but the rest of him remained motionless. His eyes grew two sizes.

"Randa?" He finally asked.

I sensed mental talking out of my frequency. Dad hustled down the steps, took mother into his arms, and spun her around in circles. She exploded with giggles, so much like Rose, it was unbelievable. He placed a kiss on her lips before turning to face us.

They both stood in front of us, arm in arm. Our parents looked so young; they are so young compared to other parents with children our age. With us living with the Ratillians and Jahni living with the Jareneiks, they weren't much older than us. Most parents are twenty or so years older than their children are, but ours are barely thirty in age.

[Jon?] Rose asked.

[I'm okay.] I let the thought slip away.

"How did you make it home so quick?" My Dad was baffled.

"We formed an alliance!" Rose enthused.

"You… what?" He coughed.

"Well, Jon did!" She spewed.

Everyone's attention shifted to me.

"It was no big deal." I shifted my gaze around and then stared past them. I didn't like all of the attention. I was more content to watch.

"Yes, it is." Rose continued.

[Rose.] I growled.

[I am proud of you and they should be too!]

That was hard to argue with. [I guess.]

"How did it go with Shokten?" I asked my father in an attempt to lift the focus from me to him.

"He finally decided making war on Jade was not in his best interest." My father sighed. "I was planning to leave tomorrow to help you." He looked at my mother lovingly. "I wanted to go with them, but I couldn't leave with Shokten's threat."

[He always was a hothead.] Mom agreed.

[Still is.] Dad thought to us. Dad's gaze shifted to me. "Tell me about this alliance."

"Jon is the official Zellian ambassador to Drex." Rose cheered.

Jahni's smile faltered. "Drex!"

I nodded.

"How?" Jahni wanted to know.

Rose waited patiently for me to claim my glory.

"I just made a few friends." I shrugged my shoulders.

Jahni giggled. "That simple, huh?"

"Mostly, yeah." I nodded my head.

Rose rolled her eyes. "He is not explaining very well." She hooked her arm through mine. "Come on, I'm hungry." She drug me inside and everyone followed.

28

"Did Adam have something else to do? Why isn't he here?" Dad asked.

"What are you talking about?" I asked as I grabbed some food off the table.

"We haven't seen Uncle Adeam since the Zanxtear Race." Rose commented.

Dad was alarmed.

"Is that a problem?" Mom looked deeply into my father's disturbed eyes.

He said something to Mom, and she was alarmed too. "Adam was supposed to assist you to Drex in a second ship like he did Jahni and Joseph when they came to Ratilles for you."

"We haven't seen him Dad." My voice echoed disturbed caution.

"He was supposed to follow you to MaCownia." Dad replied.

"We need to find his last location immediately." Jahni

spoke fervently. "Have you talked to Aunt Delphie?"

"No. Excuse me." Dad got up and left the room.

We all sat there waiting, too confused to speak. He was back within minutes. Our eyes immediately turned to him.

"She hasn't heard anything from him in over two weeks." My father was solemn.

The devastation was just beginning to sink into all of us. We sat there in stunned silence. This was not like Uncle Adeam at all. He knew how to get information from even the most unwilling sources while keeping in touch here. He wasn't stupid enough to be caught on MaCownia. He was too careful to walk into a trap.

"Where do we look?" I exhaled.

I heard the front door slam closed and footsteps rush across the floor. Jasmine came to a sudden halt beside Dad. Her face was smooth. Her eyes were alert.

"Where is he?" Jasmine demanded.

Check out my page on Facebook!

https://www.facebook.com/Heidi-Harris-510080442485714/?

ref=bookmarks

Heidi Harris' books are on Amazon!

https://www.amazon.com/Heidi-Harris/e/B01758LK4E?

ref=sr_ntt_srch_lnk_3&qid=1591557444&sr=1-3

Zelle Saga

Zelle

Deltik

Book 1: Reality
Book 2: Dreamer
Book 3: Intervention
Book 4: Drex
Book 5: Despondent
Book 6: Stranded
Book 7: Rose
Book 8: Traitor?
Book 9: Jasmine
Book 10: Talgital
Book 11: Again
Book 12: Retired
Book 13: War
Book 14: Captured

Jareneiks

Drex